Struck

EMMA LOUISE

Struck

FLAWED LOVE
BOOK THREE

EMMA LOUISE

Editing and Interior Design by Silla Webb at Masque of the Red Pen

Cover Designed by Mary Ruth at Passion Creations

Dedication

For Cornelia

That opening line though...

"In the bones of me is a better man than this."

-Tyler Knott Gregson

TJ

I recognize the light tinkle of laughter that floats across the garden toward where I'm sitting.

Lucy.

I don't have to turn and look at her to know she'll have a captivating smile on her face, and her cheeks will be flushed a fucking adorable shade of pink. She's probably using her hands to swipe away at the tears her laughter will no doubt bring on.

I don't have to look at her to know, but I do anyway.

My eyes find her immediately. She's standing on the back deck of my brother's house, just a few feet away from me, her long dark hair blowing gently around her face. She's still the most beautiful woman I've ever seen.

I've made so many mistakes with her. We both have. Despite it all, I've never been able to forget her.

One night.

That's all we've shared. One night where she made me feel more than I've ever felt before. One night that scared me stupid and had me running.

"This was a mistake."

The look on her face when I lied to her with those words will forever be burned into my mind.

In all the years that have passed, in all the ways we've lashed out and hurt one another, I've never, not once, not wanted her. It didn't matter when she tried to make me jealous. It didn't matter when she ignored me or got so mad I thought she'd never speak to me again. It didn't matter when she thought I was sleeping with anything that moved.

None of it matters, not when there's no one else who has ever come close to making me feel what she does.

She stands there, hands waving as she talks to my sister-in-law, completely unaware of me. Poppy laughs at whatever crazy story she's telling this time. My nephew, Chase, joining in with them, even if he obviously has no idea what they're talking about.

My body burns with the effort it takes to stay in my seat, when all I want to do is pull her into my arms and show her exactly how wrong I was before. It's not that I haven't tried. Lord knows how I've tried, but it's never been enough.

"I hate who I am when I want you."

The memory of the last time I begged her to listen to me sits sour in my gut. The finality in her words like a knife twisting in an open wound.

Draining the beer I've been holding on to for the last hour, I walk slowly toward where everyone is standing. Taking my time because I need a minute to get the armor in place. My steps falter as I hear the glass doors at the back of the house side open. Anger poisons my veins as I watch him walk out onto the deck.

The reason I haven't spoken to Lucy in months. The reason I stay away.

He makes his way toward her, stopping quickly to shake hands with my brother as he stands at the grill. He kisses Poppy on the cheek and makes Chase squeal with laughter with one quick tickle.

No matter what shit we pulled with each other over the last year, there's never been anyone serious for me. Never anyone serious for her. Until this guy. When I thought she was with Hayden, I was filled with jealousy. But seeing her with Scott, I quickly realized that she's finally found what she's been looking for.

And it's not me.

Frozen in place, I watch as he slides an arm behind Lucy's waist, pulling her into his side. Jealousy roars through me when I see the way she smiles at him. Has she ever looked at me like that? Or has it always been scowls and disgust on her face?

I only look away when I see his face move closer to hers.

"I'm out," I announce as the loud smash of my beer bottle hitting the bottom of the trash can fills the air.

"We haven't even eaten yet!" Poppy cries.

"Sorry, lolly-pop. Places to go, people to do." I smirk at her, but I know she sees through the bullshit. She sees past the mask. She gives me one of her quiet, assessing looks, but she doesn't say anything straightaway. I'm fucking glad, because I'm not sure I can hold my temper if she starts pushing me about why I'm really leaving. I distract her by stealing Chase from her arms, bringing him close to my chest so I can get a slobbery kiss from him. Making sure I get a bigger laugh from him before I pass him off to my brother.

I somehow manage to say goodbye to Lucy without throwing her over my shoulder and taking her home with me. I even manage to give her boyfriend a back slap as I say my goodbyes. Seems like I can pretend that I don't give a fuck with the best of them.

It's not until I make it to my truck that I release the breath that's been choking me. Slamming the gear stick into first, I speed away from the house and the piece of myself I just left behind, wrapped up in another man.

Instead of pulling into the nearest bar like I'd planned to, I keep driving.

The more miles between Lucy and me the better. I drive until the need to numb myself wins out.

Pulling over and parking outside the first bar I see, I quickly make my way inside, where I unknowingly fuck up my life even more than it already was before.

One

TJ

"It's okay. You don't have to love me."

The voice is a nothing but a whisper that cuts through the dark of my bedroom. I don't know if it's a memory or a figment of my` imagination.

Maybe it's a ghost, or maybe I'm just losing my fucking mind.

All I know is that voice; those words have been haunting me for months now. Every time I try to sleep, it's there. When I close my eyes, I see the tear-filled eyes. The lips that tremble ever so slightly before they say those fucking words.

Dark hair that hangs over us like a veil.

Soft lips, smooth skin.

No words, just sounds.

No words until I say her name. No, not her name.

"It's okay. You don't have to love me."

Scrubbing my hands over my face, I lay and stare at the dark ceiling for a while until I can't stand my thoughts any longer. Rolling to my side to look at the clock on my nightstand, I see it's just after four am. It's pointless trying to sleep now, so I throw the tangled blankets off my legs and get up. My body screams in protest as I move. I'm fucking sick of waking up like this. Bruised everywhere and pissing blood half the time. I shouldn't have fought again tonight. I've not been giving myself time to heal properly.

Throwing a coffee pod into the Keurig, I don't move away until it's ready. Not bothering to let it cool down, I swallow it down in a few gulps. I stand with my back to the small kitchen island and try to look out the window, but the sun is nowhere near ready to rise yet. The inky night sky means all I can see is my face reflected at me in the glass.

I barely recognize the man looking back at me. The hair that's a few months past needing a cut. The dark circles under my eyes that aren't just from sleepless nights. Running a hand over the scruff lining my jaw, I feel the swollen skin beneath. I press hard on the tender spot and relish the sharp stab of pain the action brings. The longer I look at myself, the more anger begins to seep through me. Anger at who I've become. Anger that I've become the kind of guy who would use one woman to help him get over another.

It's okay, you don't have to love me. Just give me tonight.

By the time I'm walking into Flex that afternoon, I'm already dragging ass. Instead of going back to bed and trying to get some sleep, I'd hit the gym in my apartment building. I never workout here anymore. In fact, I avoid this place as much as possible. It's just too fucking hard. Everywhere I look, she's there. Even when she's not in the building, her energy is. I just hope like fuck that I don't see her here today.

I make it to my office without seeing her and let out the breath I've been subconsciously holding. Unlocking the door, I let myself take in the dusty room. Has it really been that long since I've been here? I don't even remember the last time, if I'm honest with myself.

I don't get the chance to sit before the door opens behind me, my brother stepping into the room. Keir is another person I really didn't need to see today.

"Didn't expect you in today." No hello. No how've you been. I don't bother looking up at him, hoping he'll take the hint and leave me alone.

"Didn't realize I had to check-in with you," I reply with more bite than I'd like to have used.

"Don't be a dick," he replies, but there's no heat behind his words. He just sounds tired. Taking a look at him, I see he doesn't just sound tired. He looks it too. We might be twins, but we don't look much alike outside of us both having the same dark hair. "I'm not here to fight with you."

"Why are you here then?"

I wish I had a reason for why I've been determined to cut them all out. I don't. Somewhere along the line it just became easier to stop being around them all. I didn't have to pretend I was okay if I stayed away.

"Do you have time to talk?" Do I have the time? Yes. Do I want to talk to him? Fuck no.

"I just came in to grab some stuff. I'm not staying." His jaw clenches with frustration, and part of me wishes he would hurry up and call me out on my crap. I'd have lost patience with him a long time ago if the roles were reversed.

"Make time. Soon." He doesn't bother to look my way before he moves toward the door. "We need to talk about this place."

"What about it?" Flex is my baby. I came up with the idea to open it. A middle school obsession with wrestling turned into a teenage love of all things MMA. I'd been on the edge of going pro when a torn rotator cuff put me on the side-lines. With fighting no longer an option, I'd taken up training at my old gym. Anything to be involved in the sport. When my brother retired from the NFL, I asked him if he wanted in. It was more reason for him to move back to Savannah than anything else. I didn't need his help, and I definitely didn't need him trying to take over.

He turns to answer me, and I can see he's had enough. The frustration on his face has morphed into anger.

"You're not here," he snaps. "When you are here, you might as well not be. Somewhere along the way, you stopped giving a shit. About Flex, about your family. About yourself." I don't argue with him. He's right.

"You're fighting again." It's a statement, not a question.

Gritting my teeth, I don't bother to reply. It's obvious, the bruises speak for themselves. "Flex is ready to expand, to grow into the very thing you wanted it to be, but I'm sick of waiting for you to catch up. Sick of waiting for you to give me a few minutes of your time. Sick of you risking it all for the thrill of an illegal fight."

He pauses before saying the last thing I expected to hear from him, "Let me buy you out."

"What the—" the words explode from somewhere deep inside me, and before I know it, I'm on my feet, standing nose to nose with my brother. The guy that I thought would have my back, always.

"This place is mine," I grit out, "and I'll be dragged out of here swinging before I let you take it from me."

"You don't give a shit, T." My hands fist in his shirt as I yank him closer to me. Keir is a big guy. Years of playing pro football, followed by running a gym mean he's in great shape. Usually I'd say it would be hard to pick a winner between us in a fight. But right now, he doesn't have the same kind of anger fueling him that I do. Anger that's masking the small warning voice inside my head that's telling me not to do something I might regret soon.

"This place is mine." I repeat through clenched teeth. "Don't push me on this." He doesn't flinch, though. His always calm demeanour still in place, eyes quietly assessing me.

"If you care this much. Start showing it." He pushes my hands off his shirt, still sounding completely unaffected. "I'm sick of running this place alone." He looks at me as if he's debating with himself over something. "Poppy is pregnant."

A long-forgotten warmth hits me. I know they've been trying for another baby since my nephew was born eighteen months ago. I'm such a prick. I can't remember the last time I saw Chase. He probably doesn't even remember me. The fight drains right out of me, leaving me to sink into the seat behind my desk.

"Congratulations. I know you've wanted this for a while."

"She's three months along." I don't know if he means it to, but the words seem like an accusation. Three months. Has it been that long since I've seen them? I've spoken to our parents here and there, but I know this is news Keir would have wanted to tell me face to face.

The silence hangs heavy around us.

"You know I came back here for you." He sighs. "You sold me this idea of us being a team, working together, and I bought it. But us being a team, that doesn't just mean in here." He stabs a finger into the desk. "It means we're here for each other all the time. How would you feel if I'd have cut you out when Pop left me all those years ago?" Keir and Poppy had their fair share of hard work trying to get to where they are now, including a ten-year separation. The first year after she left was brutal. Our parents and I had had to stand on the sidelines while he fought his demons. Demons that included too much booze and too many women. It hits me hard how wrong I've been to shut them all out. Memories of how it felt to watch him struggle, how frustrating I felt that I couldn't help him, hit me hard.

"I'm sorry." The words stick in my throat. Running a hand over my face just to give myself a minute to think of how to explain things to him. When I don't speak, Keir drops into the seat in front of me.

"I don't need an apology. I just want you to let me in, let us all in."

"I didn't know how to deal with it. With seeing her." I don't have to say her name. Keir knows who I'm talking about. "It was easier to stay away. And then..." I let the words die instead of finishing.

"Then, what?" There's only concern in his question, no judgement, and fuck if that doesn't make me feel even more guilty. I think I prefer dealing with his anger.

"And then I did some shit I'm not proud of." I'm not ready to give him more than that right now, and I know he won't push it. "I couldn't face you. Not when I couldn't even face myself most days."

"She's happy. You know that, right?" His words sting, but they don't pack the same punch they would have just a few months ago. I want that for her. Would I rather her be happy with me? Of course, but I fucked up, and now I have to deal with it.

"He's good to her?" I ask, bracing for his answer.

"Treats her like a queen." There's no hesitation in his answer. There isn't anything I can say to that, so I don't even try to answer.

We sit in the heavy silence for a beat. Keir is the one to break it. "You done hiding from us now?" I want to be, so I nod.

"I'll do better. I'll *be* better," I promise him and myself. I really fucking hope it's a promise I can keep.

"There's good things happening around you, brother. Wake up and be a part of them. Chase misses you. We all miss you."

TJ
Three months later

Spotting an empty parking space right outside the hospital, I park my truck and shut off the engine. Pulling my phone out of the holder, I check Keir's message again, telling me what room Elliott is in. I'm stalling. I don't want to be here, not when I know that it's pretty much guaranteed I'm going to be in the same room as Lucy.

The last few months I've seen her around. We've spent time together in the same group, nights out, family parties. Now that I'm back at the gym full time, we have no choice but to be civil to one another. We have avoiding each other down to a fine art, only speaking when absolutely necessary. I'm still not sure how I feel about that, but I'm dealing with it instead of running away from it, and that's progress in my book.

As much as I'd like to not be here today, Poppy's brother and his wife just had a baby, and this is me proving to my brother that I can give a shit about other people. If I'm being honest, it's about proving it to myself too. Grabbing the small blue bear from the seat next to me, I get out and lock the doors behind me.

Five minutes later and I'm lost. I've taken a wrong turn somewhere. I fucking hate hospitals. Too many sports-related ER trips as a kid. The smell alone is enough to make me wish I was anywhere else right now.

Standing in a corridor full of closed doors, I'm five seconds away from going home. Or the bar. Anywhere that isn't here.

"What the fuck are you doing here?" a voice growls from the side of me. Turning around I see a woman who's vaguely familiar stepping out of the small family room I just walked past. Her hard, angry eyes are trained on me as I look over my shoulder to see if she's talking to someone else behind me, but it's just us out here.

"Excuse me?"

"You heard me. You're not welcome here. I have no idea who the hell told you to come here—"

Confusion turns to anger. I have no idea what she's talking about, but her tone is pissing me off. She's moved so she's standing right in front of me. I'm a big guy, and there's not a lot of full-grown men that would step up to me like this, but this tiny woman doesn't give a shit. She has no problem getting in my face.

"I don't know what the fuck your problem is, but—"

"Hey." A nurse steps in between us both, her hands up ready to push either of us back if needed. "This is not the time or place for this. You both need to leave."

"I'm not leaving. This crazy person just attacked me for no reason," I say, planting my hands on my hips.

"You're not welcome here. You're not needed here. I can't believe they fucking called you." Her voice cracks, and she looks seconds away from tears, but she steels herself and keeps on speaking. "Anyway, you're too late." Whatever is going on is obviously hard for her. Taking her in now that she's not in my face, she looks exhausted, like she hasn't slept in days. She's obviously going through some stuff, and seeing her about to break down calms my own anger. The nurse is still standing there between us, trying to decide if she needs to call security or not.

"Look, I think you've got me confused with someone else. I'm just here to visit a friend who just had a baby."

"Friend," she scoffs, interrupting me. "Wasn't very friendly of you to abandon her when she needed you most."

"Okay, crazy lady, that's enough. I'm out of here." I turn to make my way down the corridor, stopping next to the nurse as I go. "You might want to get security down here for this one." She looks between us once again, obviously having no idea what the fuck to make of the last few minutes.

"Walking away again, TJ? Good at that, aren't you?"

My steps falter at her use of my name. Heat prickles at the back of my neck, almost like I can feel the anger in her stare. This whole thing is pushing my patience to its already frayed limits. I swing around, and within a few strides I'm back in her face.

"How do you know my name, and what the fuck is going on?" I feel like I'm in a parallel universe right now. She doesn't back down. No, this girl is fearless. Jaw ticking, feet planted in place, she leans back to look me up and down, not in the way women usually do, though. No, her gaze is full of disdain.

"Willow was right about you," she says with venom dripping from each word.

Venom that I feel seep through me from where the words have landed. That name. I only know one woman with that name.

Willow.

I've spent months feeling like a prick over how I treated her.

Willow, the one-night stand that haunted me. The one that was the wake-up call I needed. I can't say I've thought about her much since I've been back on my feet. She's a blur in my memories. Just like she was that night; I remember being with her, but it's a shadow of a memory at best.

"What does Willow have to do with this?"

"Nothing anymore. Willow is dead," she answers with tears leaking from her tired eyes.

Shit.

My eyes slide closed as I take in a deep breath. I don't know how this makes me feel. We had one night. One fucked up night. I might not remember it in much detail, but I do know she used me as much as I used her. I might have been fighting demons, but she'd been fighting a few of her own. Opening my eyes, I see she's staring at me. Her eyes assessing me, looking for something.

"You didn't know? I thought that's why you're here."

"I had no idea. I really am here to see a friend who just had a baby." She seems to flinch slightly at my words. Her arms that are covered by a too big hoodie rap around her middle, like she's curling in on herself.

"I'm really sorry," I say quietly, but she doesn't give me a chance to keep speaking.

"She's dead." Her voice cracks as she speaks the one sentence that I never expected to hear. The one sentence that completely rocks the ground beneath my feet.

"She's dead, but your son is alive and in the NICU"

TJ

My son?

The world dips and tilts on its axis. Whatever she sees on my face must let her know how fucked up I'm feeling because she actually looks guilty for blurting it out like that. She's saying something, but all I hear is my blood rushing in my ears.

My son. Is it possible?

"Is he ... uh ... is he ok?" I ask the woman whose name I still don't know, but it's the nurse who speaks. She looks at me but directs her words to the lady that's looking at me like she's not sure what I'm about to do next.

"Jessie, is this Abel's father?" she asks softly.

"Abel?" I ask stupidly. My son, Abel.

I have a son, and his name is Abel.

Jessie doesn't say anything, just nods. I look back toward the nurse, and she looks at me with sympathy staining her expression.

"He's going to be fine. Abel is a strong boy," she says, trying to reassure me. "Why don't we go sit down, and I'll tell you a bit more about how he's doing?"

"You said he's fine, what else is there to tell me?" A wave of panic hits me from out of nowhere. Five minutes ago, I had no idea he existed; now I'm terrified something is going to happen to him.

"Abel is going to be fine. Please, sit down, and I'll explain everything to you." She guides me to a chair, and Jessie sits a few seats away from me. The nurse introduces herself, telling me her name is Louisa and she's been looking after Abel since he was born a few days ago by emergency c-section.

"Willow came in because she'd been feeling unwell for a few days. After running some tests, the doctors decided it was best to deliver the baby right away. She had something called pre-eclampsia. Usually the baby being born is enough to bring down mom's blood pressure, and they'll feel back to normal pretty much straightaway. Unfortunately, Willow had a seizure a few hours after she was brought back from recovery. They did everything they could to help her." I drop my head into my hands trying to listen as she speaks, but it's too much. All of this is too much.

Willow went through all that alone.

The thought keeps running through my head. She must have been so scared. Louisa stands, telling me she'll go find out if I can visit with Abel yet. When the door closes behind her, we're left in silence. I have too many things fighting for space in my head, too many questions that need answering.

"Was she alone?" I ask the room.

"I brought her in and stayed with her," Jessie speaks quietly. "She got to see Abel for a while, held him too. She was awake after the section, and I thought she was going to be okay." More tears leak from her eyes. "Then she said she didn't feel right, so the nurses came and took the baby so she could rest. I thought she was just tired. I was about to leave, let her get some sleep, but she started shaking. I don't know what happened, but one minute she was there, the next she was gone." Jessie sobs. The sound of it is killing me. Moving closer, I pull her into my side. I'm surprised she lets me after being on the receiving end of her anger earlier.

"Why didn't she tell me? Did she even try?" I have to ask. I can't work out why Willow wouldn't want me involved. Jessie sniffs as she pulls away from me. "It was a few months after you guys met that she realized she was pregnant. It took a long time for her to get her head around the fact that she was going to have a baby. Every time I told her she had to tell you, there was an excuse. She only had your first name and, in the beginning, said she couldn't find you." Jessie looks at me before she continues to speak; it's as if she's not sure if she wants to go on. "When she was about six months, she came home one day and told me she'd found you, but you wanted nothing to do with her or the baby. She said she was going to do it alone. She doesn't have family, so I told her we'd be okay, that I'd be there for them."

"I never saw or spoke to her." Anger crowds my thoughts. I would have never, not in any situation, told her that. Why did she lie?

"I guessed by your reaction that you didn't have a clue what I was talking about. I'm sorry for attacking you like that. I just assumed."

"Don't apologize for looking out for them. I don't understand why, though? I admit I was drunk that night, but did I hurt her? What did I do to her?"

Jessie doesn't get to answer me before Louisa is back to tell me I can go see the baby. My baby. I'm on my feet and following behind her before I can think too much about how insane this whole situation is. There'll be time to freak out later.

Just before I leave the room, Jessie stops me. "You never asked."

Turning around I see she's standing now, arms back wrapped around herself.

"Asked what?"

"You never asked if he's definitely yours."

It never occurred to me that he might not be mine. The dates line up, but that means nothing. Willow could have been with anyone.

"If Willow said he's mine, then he is." Jessie gives me a weak smile.

It might make me an idiot, but I'm following my gut right now.

Once I've scrubbed my hands and rubbed them with some antibacterial gel, I'm shown a crib in the corner of the dimly lit NICU room. I'm stuck in place, too fucking scared to walk any closer. There are machines and lights everywhere. There are only five other cribs in here, none have anyone sat at them, but they all appear to have babies.

"Come on. Let's go meet your boy." A nurse appears at my side, directing me to sit. When I get a glimpse inside the clear plastic, I'm glad I'm not on my feet anymore.

I've been punched, real fucking hard, by some of the biggest guys out there. But nothing, not one thing, has ever hit me with as much force as seeing this tiny part of me in that crib does.

He's tiny. The nurse tells me he's almost five pounds, and that's amazing for being born five weeks early, but to me, he's too small. He's lying on his belly, tiny arms tucked up under his chest, legs bent at the knees. His head is covered by a knitted hat. The need to lift him out consumes me. To see his hands and feet. Check all his fingers and toes. To take his knitted hat off and run my hand over his head. I need to feel him, this perfectly formed but tiny human that these people are telling me I helped create.

"You can touch him," Louisa says as she checks the machines that surround him. "Just put your hands through that hole there."

I don't move. I don't know if I can do this, how I'm going to do this. Willow didn't want me to be part of his life. She wasn't planning to tell me about him. What if she was right? I know better than anyone just how much of a fuck-up I am.

I'm about to get up and walk away when Abel opens his eyes. He blinks sleepily, mouth opening on a wide yawn. He blinks once, twice more before he looks at me.

"Move closer, he can't focus far right now. Let him see you," Louisa urges me.

"He doesn't know me. I don't want to scare him," I whisper. "I've not been there for him, for his mom."

"That's the amazing thing about babies." She smiles at me. "They are a blank slate. He doesn't know anything about mistakes made in the past, just the fact that you're here now."

Moving my chair as close to the crib as possible, I take a few deep breaths before leaning closer to him. I gently place my hand in the crib next to his head, using my finger to stroke the back of his hand.

Until this moment, I've been a mess of conflicting feelings. Shock and helplessness being the two most predominant, but the second his tiny fingers unfurl from the fist they were in to wrap around mine, everything stops. His glassy gray eyes lock on mine, and I have no idea if he can see me, but it doesn't matter. I see him.

I have no idea what the future holds. No idea how I'm going to do this, but I know I'm going to do everything this little boy needs me to do.

"You'll be able to hold him a little later. He's pretty much regulating his own temperature now; Doctor Fernandes wants to see how he does over the next few hours."

"Hold him? I'm not—"

"The best way for you guys to bond is for you to do as much skin on skin contact as possible. We'll be here with you the whole time. You're not alone," Louisa assures me.

I'm not going to be alone. I know my family will be there, it's what we do. I just have no idea how to tell my family that I've fucked up. Yet again.

Pulling my phone out of my pocket with the hand that Abel isn't holding, I unlock it. Ignoring the many missed calls and texts from Keir, I open the camera and take some pictures of him. My mom is going to want to see these as soon as I tell her about him.

It's not long before his eyes start to close again. When his grip on my finger loosens, I move my hand to rest on his back, mesmerized by the feel of his soft skin. The hypnotic, gentle rise and fall as he breathes.

Pulling myself away from him is so fucking hard. I'd happily spend the rest of time sitting here with him, but I need my family here. I don't want them to miss this.

Letting Louisa know that I'll be in the waiting room if Abel needs anything, I step out into the hallway. It's then I realize Jessie isn't there. I'll have to make sure to find her and say thank you for everything she did for Willow and Abel. I'm sure part of her still hates me, but I'll just have to prove her wrong by being the best father I possibly can be.

Shutting the waiting room door behind me, I drop down into one of the empty chairs ready to call my brother. Maybe I should call my mom and dad first, but I'm hoping I can get him in my corner before I tell them. I have his name up on the screen and quickly press the call button before I can talk myself out of it. It barely rings twice before he answers. "You okay?" No judgement. Despite being a fuck for most of the last year, and letting him down again today, my brother's first reaction is still to make sure I'm okay.

"Where are you?" I ask, ignoring his question.

"Just about to leave the hospital."

"I'm here. Inside the hospital." Unexpected emotion fills me, choking the words I'm trying to say. I can't do this over the phone. "Can you, uh … Can you guys come back in here. I need you here."

I steel my emotions and tell him I'm at the NICU. He doesn't ask any questions, only assures me he's headed back before he hangs up. Instead of waiting for them here in the waiting room, I go stand outside the NICU. Looking through the window, I can see his crib, but he's so small I can barely make him out.

The door at the end of the hallway pushes open, and Poppy rushes in, closely followed by Keir. Any other day I'd make fun of how she practically waddles down the hallway. Her pregnant belly is massive. I just don't have it in me to joke right now.

Poppy pulls me into a hug. "What's going on? Why are you here?" she asks, and I have no idea where to start. Looking at my brother, I struggle to find the words to tell him.

"Just start at the beginning. Whatever is going on, we'll help you," Keir says, dropping a reassuring hand on my shoulder. Taking a deep breath, I tell them everything. From the time I left their house all those months ago. How I drove around until stopping in that bar. How I'd already been drunk when Willow and her friends, one I now realize was Jessie, had come into the bar. I tell them how she seemed as lost as me. I'd been looking to escape my feelings for Lucy, and Willow had her own problems she was trying to drown out. I tell them that I was so fucking drunk that I barely even remember us having sex. I recall waking up in my truck the next day, outside the bar with Willow already gone. That was a low point, even for me.

Finally, I tell them about today. About the mind fuck that was walking into this hospital only to be confronted by Jessie with the news that I have a son. Poppy covers her mouth to stop a gasp falling out. Keir closes his eyes and his jaw tightens, but he doesn't say a word.

"Is he okay? The baby?" Poppy asks, her eyes flitting over to the NICU sign on the wall.

"He's good, but he was born a few weeks early so has to stay in there while he grows some." Swallowing down the lump that forms in my throat, I carry on. "Willow, his mom ... she ... uh ... she had something wrong with her blood pressure. Pre-something or other ... I don't know." I struggle to get the words out, the reality of them hitting me hard. "They delivered the baby early so they could help her get better, but it didn't work. She died yesterday." Poppy gasps, but I don't see it because my brother wraps his arm around my shoulders before I even get the words out, like he knew what I was going to say. That's all it takes for me to break. Tears that have been simmering inside me for the last few hours break free. I don't recall the last time I cried, but today, it's just all too fucking much.

I cry for Willow. For how scared she must have been going through what she did all on her own. Not knowing she'd be leaving Abel.

I cry for Abel, knowing he'll have to grow up without a mom.

I cry for me because I have no idea how the fuck I'm going to raise him on my own.

Four

TJ

"Yes, Mom, I'll call you as soon as the doctor has been around."

"I'm not kidding, Theodore." My mom just full named me. If I wasn't trying to get her to take me seriously, I'd laugh at her.

"Seriously, Mom. As soon as he gets his check-up, I'll call you and Dad right away." I can practically hear her eyes rolling at me down the phone. "I gotta go. He's going to be ready for a feed any minute."

"Okay, sweetie. Give my grandson a kiss for me, please."

"You know I will, Mom. Speak to you soon." I hang up before she can get another word in. Tucking my cell into my pocket, I push open the NICU door. It's been two weeks since I found out about Abel. Two weeks of watching him grow and change right before my eyes.

After explaining the situation to Keir that day, he and Poppy stayed by my side while I spoke with Abel's doctors. They explained that they were happy with his overall health, but he needed time to put on weight and to learn to regulate his body temperature. Abel must have been listening because right from that first day, he's been growing like a weed.

I'll never forget the first time they let me hold him. The nurses sat me in a chair next to his crib and told me to take my shirt off before handing me a tiny, sleeping Abel. I don't think I took a full breath the whole time he was in my arms, scared of the monitors still attached to him.

Feeling his skin on mine was like nothing I'd ever experienced. The only possible way to describe it is that I felt everything holding Abel for the first time. I was terrified of hurting him. Scared of what the future might hold. Could I keep him safe? Be the dad he would need me to be? Bigger than the fear was the overwhelming love, something I had never experienced. Holding him cradled to my chest, I got so fucking mad at myself. Mad at who I had let myself become in the past, at all the stupid mistakes I'd made. One hand holding his diaper-covered butt, the other cradling the back of his tiny head, I could only hope that those days are behind me, that going forward I'll be a man that one day he'll be proud of.

Telling my parents was one of the hardest things I've had to do, but I should have known they wouldn't be anything less than supportive. Mom has been making sure my place is ready for a baby, and I can't thank her enough because I have no idea what I'm doing.

The nurses in the NICU greet me as I make my way to Abel's crib. I've been here with him every day, only leaving to shower and eat, so I've gotten to know them all pretty well. When I get to Abel, he's fast asleep. It doesn't look like he's moved since I left him an hour ago. He's grown so much, he doesn't look like the same baby. His face has filled out, and his round cheeks are so cute. He looks like me. It's crazy, but he does. Soft, dark hair covers his head, and his gray eyes look like they're turning a shade of brown, just like mine.

I have no idea what color Willow's eyes were. The thought is a kick in the junk. I've had a lot of time to think about her these last few weeks. I barely remember her. My son was conceived while I was blackout drunk. The very few bits of that night I do remember make my skin crawl. All I have are flashes of memories. My hands touching her, trying to convince myself that she was Lucy. I've cycled through hurt, anger, and sadness multiple times, trying to work out why she wasn't going to tell me about him. I think I understand it, though. Watching my son sleeping without a care in the world, I want his life to be like that for as long as possible. I see it from her perspective. Why would she want some drunk asshole in her baby's life? No, I can't be angry at her.

Just myself.

Shame squeezes at my chest.

Before I can fall too far down the self-pity black hole, Abel's doctor comes in. This is what I've been waiting for. They say if he's put on enough weight, he can come home tomorrow. The thought half terrifies me, but I know we need to get on with our lives. The sooner we get home and settled, the better things will be for both of us.

An hour later and he's passed all his tests with flying colors. We can go home tomorrow.

I try to pass time by packing up some of his stuff while he's napping. It's amazing how much crap one little person needs. I'm almost finished when the door opens, and my brother and his wife walk through. I'm not surprised. Between them and my parents, Abel and I have had visitors every day. Even Lucy has been in to visit. I can't say it wasn't awkward as fuck, but right now, all I care about is making sure Abel has what he needs, even if all he needs right now is my time and attention.

"Look at him!" Poppy gushes, leaning over the side of his open top crib. "He looks more and more like Chase every time I see him."

"That's because the Harmon genes are strong," Keir answers, leaning over and kissing Abel on the head.

"Speaking of that little terror, where is my nephew?"

"Your mom called this morning. Said you banned her from coming up here today, and she needed a distraction."

"So you have a child-free day and you choose to come here?"

"We had an appointment upstairs; this one is determined to be the biggest baby ever born." Poppy groans as she rubs her hands over her huge belly.

"Not long now." Keir rubs her shoulder. The easy way they have with each other doesn't go unnoticed by me.

"What did the doctors say? When is he getting out of here?"

"Tomorrow morning, he'll be a free man." The smile on my face is genuine, but he studies me, making sure I'm as happy as I'm saying I am.

"You good?" It's an innocuous question, but I know he's asking so much more than if I'm good.

"I'm good." And for once I'm not lying. My life has been chaos these last two weeks, but Abel has also brought me a sense of calm I've not had for a long time. I've got something to focus on now.

"Yeah, you are," he says, pulling me in for a hug and a back slap.

The next morning, as soon as he's cleared, I've got Abel strapped into a car seat. If I thought he looked tiny in a hospital crib, he's practically disappearing in this seat. He's barely visible between the blankets tucked tight around him and the hat that's pulled low on his head.

The nurses have all been stopping by to say goodbye. This kid has made quite an impression on everyone here. My mom and dad are here to help me get him home and settled. They wanted us to stay with them, but I figured we'd be better just getting him home.

A few days after finding out about him, I set my mother the task of finding me a house to move into. The shitty apartment I'd lived in for the last few years is in no way suitable for a kid. My mom lost her mind at me for buying a house without seeing it, but I trust her. Between my friends and family, they've got the new place decorated, ready for us to go home to. I'm pretty sure my mom is going to put her foot down and demand to stay with us, at least for a little while. She won't get an argument from me. I might have been taught how to feed and burp him, keep him clean, the basic stuff. But I've no idea how we'll be when we get home.

No, I'll take all the help I can get, thank you very much.

Once we're all packed up, the other parents that are here with their babies make sure to say goodbye to us. It's strange, but you form a bond with these people. They understand the highs and lows that come with being in here. One of the mothers pulls me in for a hug. "I'm not going to lie, I'm sure going to miss seeing you with no shirt on holding that baby." A loud laugh burst's out of me. Lily gave birth to triplets almost three months before their due date. I've never seen anything as small as those little boys. She's also married to a great guy who looks at her like she hung the moon, so I take her words exactly as the joke she meant them to be.

"Yeah, yeah. I'll miss you guys too. Tell Matt to call me when he's ready for that gym time."

With our goodbyes said, I carry my son outside for the very first time.

I have no idea what the future holds for us, but for the first time in a long time, I have something to look forward to.

BREEZE

Three months later

"No, no, no!" My piece of shit car shutters a few times before it lurches forward. I flip the signal when I see a parking lot just up ahead. It doesn't even surprise me when the stupid thing doesn't work. I've barely turned the corner when the engine dies. Luckily, I manage to roll it forward just enough to not be blocking the entrance.

"Fuuuck!" I groan, dropping my head to the steering wheel. This can't be happening. Not today. Yanking my phone out of my purse, I pray that I remembered to charge it for once.

Six percent. Hell yes.

At least one thing seems to be going my way. Scrolling through my recent call list, I click on my oldest brother's name. "Come on. Answer please," I murmur to myself. Looking at the clock, I see it's almost ten a.m. There's no way I'm going to be on time now. I just have to try and hope they'll still see me a little later than we agreed. I'm about to hang up the phone when he answers.

"It's the middle of the night. What you want?" He sounds like he's been chewing gravel.

"Asa. It's ten in the morning."

"Well, we only just got to bed, so it's the middle of the night for me."

"We?" I ask but immediately regret it. "Wait, don't tell me. I really don't want to know." My brother gives new definition to the term man whore. His deep laugh rumbles down the phone, making my lips tip up into a smile.

"No, little sis, you really do not wanna know."

"One day, big brother. One day you'll be sorry when you finally meet the one, and you have to explain your man whore ways."

"You call me to talk shit about my bedroom habits, Breeze? 'Cause, if you're done, I can think of better ways to spend my morning now that I'm awake—"

"Stop speaking!" I shout desperately into the phone. I do not need to hear this. "My car broke down again."

"Bree, how many times do I have to tell you to scrap that piece of shit?" Thank god he can't see my eye roll down the phone.

"I know, I know. It was supposed to go in the garage this week, but ... but I have an interview this morning, and I really want this job." I beg, "Please, Asa." I'm giving him puppy dog eyes and a lip pout, even though he can't see me down the phone.

"Where are you?" He sighs, and I have to stop myself from doing a little dance in my seat as I tell him where I am.

By the time Asa pulls up outside Flex, I'm only twenty minutes late for my interview. Luckily for me he's still tired, so he's been quiet for once. I'm sure outside of bedding a new woman every night, my brother's favorite pastime is riding my ass. He's quiet until the car comes to a stop that is. Before I can get out, his hand clamps down on mine.

"Keys."

"I'll sort it once I'm done here."

"Keys, Breeze. Now." It's pointless arguing with him. Asa is the oldest of us Lucas kids at almost thirty, and he's somehow convinced he needs to play dad to us all. I make a production of slamming my key into his outstretched hand.

"This is the last time I fix that piece of shit for you. Next time I'm scrapping it," he growls at me.

"You do know I'm not a kid anymore, right? You can't actually tell me what to do." I scowl at him. As always, Asa doesn't even blink at my attitude.

"Start acting like an adult, and maybe you'll get treated like one sometimes," he jabs back.

"I am an adult, Asa, you just—"

"You're a twenty-year-old 'yoga instructor' who thinks she can get by on fairy dust and good thoughts." The cheeky fuck actually air quotes yoga instructor, like there's something wrong with what I choose to do for work. As much as I want to tell my brother to go fuck himself for his opinion, I don't. This isn't the first time we've had this conversation. I refuse to get into it again with him, especially when I'm already late.

"Let's not do this again. I don't judge you for your life choices; do the same for me. Please?"

He stares at me a beat before rolling his eyes. "You totally judge me," he mutters. He's right, I do.

"Well come on, you work security at a strip bar!"

"Nothing wrong with that, Bree."

"It's called Fuzzy Holes." I deadpan. "And you sleep with a different stripper every night."

"It's not every night," he returns.

"Doesn't matter. I still love you, even if you're a pain in my ass." I offer him a wide smile, and all I get in return is another unamused stare from him, but it's not long before he pulls me in for a kiss on my forehead.

"Love you too, Bree. Just want you safe and happy." Underneath the bad attitude and tattoos, my brother is a teddy bear.

"Dinner soon? I'll call Av and Beau? It's been forever since we had family dinner."

"I'll call them, set it up when I know my schedule for next week," he says, and just like that, Asa's tantrum is done. Until the next time I see him, at least.

Giving Asa a kiss on the cheek, I slam the car door closed before running toward the huge warehouse-style building in front of me.

Flex is huge, much bigger than I imagined. It's also the fanciest gym in town. The main doors are glass, the gym's logo etched into them; I don't want to touch them for fear of getting finger print smudges on them. Inside is just as impressive. The reception desk is massive. Everything is white or glass and super expensive looking. If it wasn't for the display of protein powders and other muscle crap, it could pass as an art gallery.

When I get to the gleaming white reception desk, it's empty. Checking the walls for a clock, I don't find one. I managed to make a quick call to explain I'd be late, but all I got was a voicemail. By now my phone is dead, so I have two choices. I can either stand here like a spare part, or I can go find whoever is supposed to be interviewing me. I figure that as it's a gym, they won't mind me wandering around a little.

The huge space is filled with exercise machines but surprisingly few people. There's an instructor helping a guy work a weight machine, and a few others running on treadmills, but that's it. Approaching the instructor, I tell him I'm here for an interview and ask if he knows where I should go. His eyes take in my outfit, and it takes everything in me not to squirm under the weight of his stare. My hands itch to pull the hem of my dress down an inch or two. I had no idea what to wear today. I'd assumed yoga pants and a tee, but when I told my sister, Avalon, she lost her mind. So here I am, wearing a floral print dress and sensible shoes. The dress seemed longer when I put it on this morning, but the way this guy is looking at my legs, I'm guessing I went too short.

"Who'd you say was interviewing you?" he asks as he finally drags his eyes up from my legs. He's a decent looking guy, like a pumped-up all-American boy next door. But the vibes he's giving off are not at all boy next door.

"The email said a Mr. Harmon? I am a little late, though."

"If you give me a minute, I'll walk you down to his office," Creepy guy offers.

"Just point me in the right direction, I'll find it." I smile sweetly, despite wanting to roll my eyes.

Armed with directions on where to find the boss' office, I hurry to find it. Making my way down the stairs, I'm surprised to see this space is just as big as upstairs, but the vibe down here is very different. There are many more people down here for a start. There's a small group of guys standing around watching the biggest man I've ever seen in my life hit a punch bag with so much force it moves back and forth as if it weighs nothing. There's also a couple of guys in a massive boxing ring dancing around each other. Two older guys are shouting orders at the fighters as they duck and weave around each other.

I don't stop to look, just keep my head down and speed-walk toward the doors at the back of the space, exactly where I was told they would be.

There are three doors, none of which have any signs. I knock on the first one, but don't get a response. The same thing happens with the second. As I approach the last door, I notice it's slightly ajar. I can hear the low murmur of voices from inside, and as much as I don't want to be rude, I really want this job. I'm about to knock when the voices start getting louder. I should go upstairs to wait, but I don't get the chance to move before the door swings open further. I step back at the same time a tall blonde woman stalks out. She's probably very pretty, but right now her face is splotched with red, and she looks like she's swallowed something nasty.

She barely takes a step out before she changes her mind, swings back around, and shouts into the open doorway.

"Next time you want your dick sucked, don't call me to do it." This time she does stomp off, her high heels clattering on the concrete floor.

I'm still staring at her retreating back when the door swings open again. A guy that steps out this time, and my first thought is that he is beautiful. Tall and built and dark. Just beautiful.

He doesn't even glance my way, just turns to call after the blonde.

"Don't worry, sweetheart, I won't be calling you. You were never very good at it anyway."

"Whatever you say, gym rat!" She yells, before she flicks him the finger over her shoulder without breaking stride, before she disappears through the doors.

Yikes, it's like I've stepped into the middle of a soap opera. He doesn't watch her leave; instead, he just turns back toward the office. I draw in a breath, about to speak when he walks straight past me, like I'm not even there. The door slamming causes the breath I was holding to squeak out of me.

Shit.

I really want this job. No, I need this job. I can't just turn around and walk out of here without at least trying to salvage this interview.

Raising a fist, I give a couple of taps on the frosted glass.

The door doesn't open, but I hear a muted "Fuck off" shouted from inside. His dismissal of me just about pushes me over the edge. I get that I was late, but to completely ignore me, to not allow me the chance to explain, is just plain rude. Especially after the little lovers spat I just had to witness. I know the right thing to do is walk away, the guys who were working out down here are now standing around watching me instead, but my stubborn streak is rearing its ugly head. I've had an awful morning. Between my car giving up, Asa being a pain in my ass, and being late, I'm fresh out of patience right now.

Instead of walking away, I lift my hand and bang the glass, harder this time. When I get no response, I do it for a third time. This time much harder again.

The door finally opens, and he fills the space in front of me. I wasn't wrong when I said he's beautiful, but somehow that doesn't do him justice. He's tall, maybe a full foot taller than my five-feet-five. Wide, strong shoulders. Muscular arms covered by a tight black tee flex as he crosses his arms over his chest. His size is certainly intimidating, but it's his face that holds my attention. Tanned skin. Deep, dark brown eyes. Heavy brows slanted down over them do nothing to hide the depths there. There's a story in those eyes. One I'd guess he doesn't share easily based on his attitude.

He's older than me for sure, but I get the feeling his serious demeanor makes him look older than he actually is. His gaze flicks from my face and over my body. He takes his time doing so, and while he's just as blatant about it as the guy upstairs, this time I don't feel the need to shy away from it. Typical of me to be attracted to the dickhead who was just having a public argument with a woman over her lack of oral skills.

Maybe Asa has a point about me needing to grow up. I don't get a chance to ponder this further, because when he's done looking me over, he finally speaks.

"I think you took a wrong turn, sweetheart. You can sign up for classes up at reception." He smirks at me, and I don't miss the faint sniggers from the guys that I'm sure have been enjoying the show they've gotten over the last few minutes.

This might be your new boss, Bree. Do not slap him.

Painting on a fake smile, I take a breath before speaking.

"I'm here to meet a Mr, Harmon?" I don't know why it comes out as a question, but it does. "I have an interview for the yoga instructor position. I'm a little late, though."

He doesn't speak. Just stands there, impassive eyes flicking over every inch of me. Even I'm starting to wonder if this job is going to be worth this much hassle. This seems like he'll be a pain in the ass to work for. I'm about to give up and leave, when the doors open once again. At first, I assume my eyes are playing tricks on me. The guy walking this way looks exactly like the moody prick standing next to me. It's not until he's made it closer to us that I see the differences between them. This new one is a touch shorter, less bulky. The biggest difference, though, is the smile on his face.

"You must be Breeze?" he asks, extending a hand toward me.

"Yes, Mr. Harmon?"

"Please, call me Keir. My office is this way." Swinging a hand toward the door furthest away from us, he waits for me to walk ahead of him. I walk away, but I do it wishing I had a reason to turn around to speak to the brooding man I'm moving away from instead.

TJ

Breeze.

The name suits her. She looks like a fucking fairy in that too short dress and all that pink hair.

Pink fucking hair.

Keir shuts his office door slightly, but I don't move away. Instead, I move closer, standing outside and listening to him ask the beautiful woman I'd just been staring at all the usual banal interview questions. She answers everything with a quiet confidence. I can imagine her face lighting up as she speaks; it's obvious from her answers that she loves what she does.

I need to get laid. One look at a pretty face and I'm turning into an idiot.

Making my way back to my office, I sit at my desk. I have so much shit to do, but today has been a disaster. Abel decided last night that he was over sleeping through the night. He must have woken me up five times. There's not enough coffee in the world to stop my ass from dragging today. But no sleep was the tip of the iceberg of shit I've had to deal. Shit I don't have time to deal with because work is also kicking my ass. Add in the visit from a crazy ex hook-up who didn't want to take no for an answer, and my day probably couldn't get any worse.

What feels like hours later and I'm finally replying to the last email that's been waiting for my attention for days now. I'm about to pick up the phone and start on the list of messages I have to return when I look at the clock, seeing it's already midday. Almost time for me to go collect Abel from my sister-in-law. Between her and my mom helping look after him, I'm able to work pretty much full time. One of the perks of owning this place, though, is that I can bring him in with me on days I'm not in the ring training someone, like this afternoon. Shutting my laptop, I get ready to collect my son. He might have kept me up all night, but I've missed him this morning.

It's crazy how much he's changed my life. Being his dad is hands down the best thing that's ever happened to me. Every day is a learning curve, but making sure he's happy, healthy, and loved is all that matters to me now. That's not to say it's been easy. Fuck no. Most of the time I don't have a clue what I'm doing. I spend so much time wondering if I'm getting it right, or if I'm raising him how Willow would have wanted me to.

That's one of the hardest parts, the not knowing. There's no link to his mother. She died with no family and only a few friends. Jessie had been back to the hospital a few times before Abel was released, but she'd been struggling with losing her friend. She let me and my family help with arranging a small funeral for Willow. After that she'd handed over a tiny box of her belongings for Abel to have. Just a few photos and her high school yearbook. After Willow was buried, Jessie had told us it was too hard for her to stay here and that she'd found work out of state. She knows she's welcome to keep in touch, to see Abel if she wants. I hope one day she feels ready to be part of his life. He's going to want to know things about his mother one day that I won't be able to answer.

When I make it upstairs, I find Poppy is already here sitting behind the reception desk, Keir leaning over kissing her. Abel is in his car seat at her feet. Once he sees me approaching, his little legs start kicking. He might have been tiny when he was born, but he's more than made up for it since he's been home. It's hardly surprising with the amount of milk the kid can put away. Almost three months old and he's already bigger than my nephew was at that age.

"What are you guys doing here? I said I'd come get him."

"I think what you meant to say is, thank you, favorite sister of mine," Poppy jokes.

"You're what, ten months pregnant now? You shouldn't be driving," I joke, causing her to roll her eyes at me.

"Hey, kid." I drop to a knee so I can unbuckle and lift him out. "You in a better mood now?" I'm treated to a gummy smile as he stretches his chubby body. Standing with him in my arms, I settle him on my hip facing away from me. He hates not being able to see what's going on.

"I think I know why this little guy had you up all night," Poppy says, giving his belly a tickle. "I'm pretty sure he's cutting at least one tooth."

I swing him around so I can take a look. He's chewing on a finger, and there's plenty of drool there. Looks like my boy's growing up. I'm not ready for this shit.

"Mind slowing down on this growing up thing, kid?" I ask him. I get a smile and few coos in reply. "Yeah, yeah, kid. I get it."

"Wanna explain what the shit was in your office this morning?" Keir asks, arms crossed over his chest.

"Nope." I ignore him. Another perk of owning this place, I don't have to explain jack shit to him.

"What happened this morning?" Poppy leans over the desk, no doubt waiting for some gossip.

"Nothing."

"Usual TJ crap." We both answer at the same time.

"Oooh! There's not been enough TJ drama lately. You're boring when you behave; you know that, right?"

"Well, I'd take boredom over him arguing with some random over her giving him a blow job," Keir mutters.

"Actually, it was about how bad she was at it." I deadpan.

"Dude. In front of my wife? Really?"

"You brought it up, not me."

"One of you better tell me what happened!"

Knowing she won't let it drop, I decide it's easier to tell her. "It was nothing. An old friend decided to drop in, and she didn't like it when I told her I wasn't interested in reconnecting." I shrug, hoping she'll leave it there. Judging by the amused look on her face, I'm betting she won't.

"Yeah, except she decided she'd share how much she didn't like it with the whole room. Including the girl I was just about to interview for the yoga instructor position."

"Ouch." Poppy laughs. "I bet that was awkward."

It wasn't, probably because I was too angry to notice her standing there.

"Well, it was awkward for me, interviewing her after that. I'd prefer it if she didn't think she was coming to work with a bunch of idiots." He huffs.

"You gave her the job?" I'm aiming for nonchalant, hoping he doesn't notice the edge that I can hear in my own voice. I shouldn't care if he gave it to her or not. I might have been attracted to her, but that means nothing. I'm not in a place in my life where I'm able to do anything about it. And anyway, I'm sure she thinks I'm trash after how we met earlier.

I tell myself this, but I can't deny the small thrill that I feel when my brother confirms that he has, in fact, offered the beautiful Breeze a job.

Seven

BREEZE

It's not until the interview is over and I'm walking out of Flex that I realize I'm stranded. No car and no phone to call anyone to pick me up. Luckily the sun is shining so the walk back isn't too hard, even if it takes over an hour. I'm going to have to get my car back on the road ASAP. Either that or I need to find a bicycle. Thinking of dipping into my savings for the car repair bill has me leaning toward the bicycle option. Especially if I get the job. Keir told me he'd be in touch once a final decision has been made, and I have everything crossed that I did enough to get this job.

Thinking of Flex inevitably has my mind wandering to those deep, dark brown eyes. Sitting there, trying to answer questions about my past work experience, it was a struggle to stay focused on my answers instead of the hot guy out in the hallway. Hopefully, I managed to wing it enough that I didn't look like an idiot.

It takes me longer than I thought, but I finally make it to Deja Brew, the coffee shop my best friend, Fleur, owns. Pushing the door open, I'm not surprised there's a line of people ten deep waiting to be served. It's like this every day. Stowing my bag under the counter, I grab an apron and tray and start collecting some of the empty mugs that litter the tables. Once my tray is full, I take them through the back so I can run the dishwasher.

"I fucking LOVE you!" Fleur shouts as I pass her. The rush doesn't die down for another few hours, and it feels like I've made a million lattes and served twice as many sandwiches. By the time it's quiet enough to take a break, it's almost four pm.

"My feet are on freaking fire," Fleur groans as she pulls out the chair next to me and sinks into it.

"That's what you get for making kick-ass coffee."

"I suppose," she grumbles. "What's with the pink hair?"

Pulling my hair out of its haphazard bun, I smooth my hands over the waves. The pink strands are bold for me. I usually leave it as the dark blonde it's always been, but the pink has grown on me. "The salon I use has a new apprentice; she cuts it for free if I let her practice her coloring techniques."

"Anything to save a buck, huh?" Fleur chuckles at me. She knows me so well. "I like it, though, looks good on you."

"You would like it." I nod at Fleur's own hair. The ends tipped a vivid blue. "Although, she said it would wash out quickly, and it's been a week already. I had that interview earlier, and I'm not sure it fit in with their style."

"What? Where was it? I thought you were looking for a new instructor position?"

"It was for that maternity cover position, over at Flex."

"I'm such a shitty friend!" she cries, slapping a hand over her eyes. "I totally forgot that was today."

"You were busy, don't even think about it." I wave her off knowing she would never purposely hurt my feelings. She's rushed off her feet running this place. Although the café is a family-run business, Fleur has been running it alone since her dad had a heart attack last summer. We've been friends since kindergarten, and the last thing she'd do is hurt me intentionally.

"Tell me how it went. I want to know all the details."

My first reaction isn't to tell her how the interview went. It's to tell her about him. Part of me wants to tell her that I met a guy that I felt instantly drawn to, but there's a bigger part that wants to keep him to myself. I don't even know his name, but standing there with him, I felt more of a connection than I'd felt after months of dating my last boyfriend. It was the craziest thing I've ever experienced.

Instead, I tell her all about the shitty start to my day, going on to give her a glossed over version of how the interview went. I'm saved from going into too much detail by the ringing of my phone over on the counter. I jump up and quickly unplug it from the charger. I don't recognize the number, but I swipe to accept the call anyway.

"Hello?"

"Hi, is this Breeze?" the deep voice I already recognize asks. "It's Keir Harmon here, from Flex." My insides jump with nerves. This needs to be good news. Please be good news.

"Hello. Hi, yes, that's me. Hi." I'm fucking babbling. I shoot a panicked gaze at Fleur but, she just laughs at me silently.

"I wanted to thank you for coming in to meet with me today." Well shit, that's not good. I feel my shoulders drop. I wanted this job so badly. I paint a fake smile on my face. He might not be able to see it, but I feel the need to fake it anyway. He keeps on speaking, but I'm paying little attention, already thinking of where else I can look for a job.

"I appreciate you giving me the opportunity," I say distractedly.

"So we were wondering if you'd be available to start next week?"

"I got the job?!" I squeak. I have to clamp a hand over my mouth to stop a louder squeal from escaping. Holy shit, I got the job! Out of the corner of my eye I see Fleur throw her hands up in the air in a silent cheer.

I get myself together enough to tell him I'll start whenever he needs me to, all the while thanking him repeatedly. Making an even bigger dork of myself than I'm sure I already have.

By the end of the call I'm practically dancing with happiness. Fleur joins me, grabbing my hands and pulling me in for a hug.

"We're going out to celebrate tonight!"

I don't argue. I just don't know if I'm celebrating the new job, or the fact that I'll soon be working so close to the guy who's been my mind way too much all day today.

TJ

Rolling over in bed, I watch Abel on the baby monitor that's on my nightstand. He's been awake for a few minutes, but he's happy babbling away to himself for now. The last few nights have been brutal with him not staying asleep for long. We hadn't long found a routine that had him sleeping for seven hours a night, but the teeth he seems to be growing have thrown him off. I never realized how hard it would be to do this alone. Hell, doing it with a partner must still be exhausting.

I take advantage of his rare good mood and quickly jump out of bed and into the shower. One skill I've picked up since being a dad is super-fast showering. I'm in and out in two minutes. By the time I have him up and in a clean diaper, Abel is making it clear that he's ready to be fed.

"I hear ya, bud," I croon as we wait for his milk to warm. He looks at me with little lips turned down in a frown. He's so fucking cute it kills me sometimes.

Once he's eaten and dressed for the day, I pack up his stuff and drive him to my mother's. Poppy is due to have baby number two soon, and Mom has been keeping both Abel and Chase while we work. I do feel some guilt whenever I drop him off, but she insists she loves her grandbabies and she'd be bored without them. I keep him with me as much as possible, but it's not always easy to focus on him and the gym at the same time. He deserves better than being stuck in my office for hours on end, and there's no way I'd be happy to put in day care while he's still so young.

After dropping Abel off, I make my way toward Flex. After avoiding the place for all those months, I'm surprised by how much I love being back there. Maybe I've gained some clarity since I've quit the booze, fighting, and partying every night. Whatever it is, I'm enjoying being back. Not only that, but Keir was right about us being ready to expand. We're beyond ready for it. Our registration numbers are through the roof, and I'm maxed out with the number of fighters I can take on. The next few months will be a challenge with me trying to do as much of Abel's care on my own and Keir adjusting to life with a newborn and a toddler. Neither of us will be able to put as much time into work as we'd like. I never thought I'd say this, but I'm grateful we have Lucy working with us. I've learned over the months to not let myself dwell on thoughts of her. I thought I'd struggle with seeing her so much, but it's been easier than anticipated to put whatever it was I felt for her in a box and lock it up. We're finally getting on, and I'm not ever tempted to dredge up old feelings. She's moved on and is happy with her guy, and I'm happy concentrating on being a dad.

A few hours later and I'm in the ring, waiting for my fighters to show up. I've just got out of a meeting to discuss some upcoming fights that mean my schedule is about to get insane.

Fucking great.

The door opens and two of my youngest guys make their way toward me, both laughing and shoving at each other.

"Bro, hands down the sweetest ass I've seen in a long time," Jonah, my best fighter, says as he dumps his gym bag and ducks into the ring. He came to me three years ago as a skinny fifteen-year-old kid with too much anger and no idea what to do to channel it. The guy with him, Danny, is new to Flex, but he's shown a lot of potential so far. "You won't hear me arguing with you on that one." They bump fists, both laughing.

These two are great kids, but I'm not in the mood to listen to their shit today. "You two ready to stop acting like horny teenagers yet?" I ask, throwing a roll of hand tape at Jonah.

"T, you would be saying the same if you were treated to the view we just got." Working in a gym, I've seen more than my fair share of attractive woman. I definitely once viewed it as a perk of the job. "Yeah, yeah. I'm sure she was hot. Now can you get warmed up? We don't have all day," I grumble.

The rest of the day passes quickly. The guys are in great form, and we've come up with some solid training plans. I am exhausted, though. Keeping up with two nineteen-year-olds isn't as easy as it used to be. I can't wait to get home, so I skip my usual shower, instead making quick work of getting everything shut down so I can leave. I end up walking upstairs behind the rest of the guys, yet again they're talking crap.

"There's no way." Danny laughs. "You are so not her type."

"Fifty bucks says I am her type, and I can get her to agree to a date by this weekend," Jonah returns.

"You do know you sound like a pair of dickheads right now, right?" I say from behind them, causing them both to turn to face me. Jonah has the decency to blush a touch. He obviously didn't realize I was there.

"We were just goofing around, T. Didn't mean anything by it." He's a good kid so I don't doubt he's just got caught up in the moment. He's not had the easiest of starts in life. His mom moved them around a lot trying to hide from his dad, so he struggled to make and keep friends. His dad eventually found them and is now serving a life sentence for killing his mom. He and his sister were raised in foster care after that. He works here part time as well as training with me as often as possible.

"Goofing around is one thing. Making bets on getting a woman in to bed is something else entirely." I've caused more than my fair share of broken hearts over the years, and I'm the last person they should be taking advice from, but here we are.

"Got it."

"You're right."

They both agree, looking sheepish.

"No more bets?" I ask.

"No bet. But I'm still askin' her out." His grin is infectious as he speaks. "I'm not kidding when I say she's smoking hot. Even with the pink hair." He walks away chuckling, Danny following close behind him. Completely unaware of the bomb he just dropped.

Pink hair. What are the odds?

I knew Keir was going to offer Breeze the instructor position, but I kept my mouth shut and didn't ask any questions. It seemed safer that way. So what if I found her attractive? Getting involved with anyone isn't on my list of shit to do anytime soon. Especially not someone as young and innocent looking as Breeze. Fuck no, I already decided I'll be ignoring her as much as possible. There have been plenty of opportunities to get laid over the past few months. I just haven't been tempted to give in to any of them. It shouldn't be difficult; there's no reason our paths should cross too often. I'll do my best to make sure of it.

So why am I suddenly itching to go see if she's still here?

Instead of giving into the urge, I put my head down and make my way to my truck. Something tells me I'm going to be spending a lot of my time avoiding the girl who's been on my mind more than I'm comfortable admitting over the last week.

I've come to find out that I was right. It would take all of my effort to avoid her. But I've also come to realize it is pointless. Staying away from Breeze is never going to be an option, not when she wouldn't let it be one.

Nine

BREEZE

Chaining up my bicycle, I jog up the steps and into Flex. I might have picked it up for practically pennies at a yard sale, but that bike means I'm not spending money on running a car so it's here to stay.

Today marks one week since I started working here, and so far, I absolutely love it. I was a bag of nerves that first day, but once Keir introduced me to Lucy and told me she'd be the one to go to if I had any issues, I immediately relaxed. It's never easy taking over an established class, people tend to find a yoga instructor they like and stick with them, but with the previous instructor at Flex going on an extended maternity leave, it was either me or they'd have to find classes elsewhere. Luckily for me, the majority opted to stick with me. I'm running ten classes a week here, and between that and picking up some shifts with Fleur, I'm exhausted.

I just have to keep reminding myself to think of the money I'm saving. The more I work, the quicker I'll be able to travel.

Dropping off my backpack in the employee room, I stop to chat with a few of the other trainers. I've been keeping to myself for the most part. I'm not anti-social as such, but making friends doesn't come naturally to me. Everyone here has been friendly enough, but I'm quite a bit younger than most. Surprisingly, one of the few people I've bonded with is the same trainer who had so blatantly checked me out the day of my interview. My first official day of work, he introduced himself and offered to show me around; this time there was no uncomfortable ogling.

That's not to say he doesn't flirt with me any chance he gets. He's relentless, but I'm sure he's just joking around. At least I hope he is.

"There she is!" Jonah announces loudly, causing everyone else in the room to turn and look at us. I feel my cheeks start to burn in embarrassment. "Let me guess, you just couldn't resist me anymore, and you're here to finally agree to a date." He grins at me, dimple on show and everything.

I can't help but laugh at his antics. Jonah is undoubtedly gorgeous. He's also funny, and something tells me that underneath all the bad boy posturing, he's actually a bit of a sweetheart. Part of me almost wishes I was attracted to him.

Leaning further toward him, I lower my voice seductively before I answer him. He's not the only one who can flirt for fun. "Not today. Not ever." He wasn't expecting me to get so close to him, and his eyes widen in shock. I can't help but laugh at the light blush on his cheeks. I'm about to move away, but before I get the chance to, a deep voice thunder's from right behind me.

"Any chance of some work getting done around here today? Or am I paying you to try to get laid?"

Turning around, I see the snide voice belongs to the guy who's been running through my thoughts way too much lately. TJ stands with his thick thighs planted wide and his huge arms crossed across his chest. My eyes eat up the sight of him, and by the time they make it to his face, I find he's staring at me, looking entirely unimpressed. His whole frame is rigid, except for the tick in his jaw.

Realizing I'm still touching Jonah, I shift away from him awkwardly. Should I apologize? Even though I know I'm not doing anything wrong, the fact that he seems to be angry at me makes me want to explain myself. Something about this moment causes an uneasy feeling to sink through me.

"I wasn't ... I mean, we were—" I stumble, trying to find the words, but he effectively cuts me off when he swings his gaze toward Jonah and speaks over me.

"You were due in the ring ten minutes ago. You think you can avoid wasting time on pointless distractions for a while?"

Ouch.

I have no idea what I've done to deserve his disdain, and I shouldn't care, but that comment hurts, nevertheless.

"Who pissed you off already this morning?" Jonah asks TJ on a laugh, before he turns and plants an obnoxiously loud kiss on my cheek.

"Gotta run before he starts cracking the whip." He even throws me a wink before turning toward the doorway where TJ stands, his stance still locked in place.

TJ doesn't move. Doesn't look at me. Not until Jonah has walked out. Once he's left, the silence he leaves behind is thick. Looking around, I realize we're the only ones left in here. Finally, his eyes swing toward me, and I'm frozen in place. I still have the urge to try to explain things to him, anything to get him to have a conversation with me. The few words we've traded have been all too brief.

It feels like we're locked in a silent battle. I just wish I knew what the fight was over. It feels like minutes since either of us have taken a breath, but it's probably no more than a few seconds. It's not until he turns to leave that I finally release some of the tension that's been gripping me. I barely make it a few steps when I see him hesitate in the doorway, just before he turns to look at me once again.

"Jonah might not have told you, but he's training hard-core right now. At least try to keep the flirting to a minimum if you can; he really doesn't need any distractions."

It's pointless trying to explain to him that he's gotten the wrong end of the stick. That he's misunderstood whatever it is he thinks he walked in on. He's made up his mind about me, and for whatever reason has decided not to like me. I'm not sure why I'm letting his obvious dislike bother me so much. So far, I've had two encounters with TJ Harmon, and both times he's acted like a dick, not letting me get a word in edgewise. Two conversations, a handful of words, and he's decided that I'm not good enough to listen to.

Well fuck him. I try not to let many things get to me, but he's pushed me too far. Before TJ can get more than a few steps down the hallway, I follow behind, calling after him.

"Be careful, you almost sound a little jealous there."

His dark gaze doesn't waver as I wait for his retort, but nothing comes. In fact, he doesn't acknowledge me at all, just turns and walks away once more.

By the time I've finished both my morning classes, I'm more than ready for lunch. I lost my appetite for breakfast after the run in with TJ this morning. Luckily the employee room is empty. I've decided it's best for everyone if I put some distance between Jonah and I for a while. It'll suck, but at least no one will be able to call me a distraction.

I quickly throw my lunch in the microwave, planning to take it upstairs to the empty studio. Hopefully if I'm quick I'll avoid bumping into anyone. I have an hour before my next class is due to start.

I'm halfway upstairs when I hear the unmistakable sound of a baby crying. Not just a cry, but a full-on wail. The sound is so out of place that I stop and listen for a second. The only small child I've seen around here is Keir's son, Chase, and he's almost two. These cries are from a tiny baby.

It's probably none of my business, but that doesn't stop me from going to see what's going on. Making my way toward the offices, the cries get louder. Passing by the rooms with closed doors, I don't bother to check them; I can already tell where the noise is coming from. And it's the last place I would have expected it to be.

Stopping outside of the slightly open door, I swipe my clammy hands down the leg of my pants. Before I can tell myself this is a terrible idea, I give the door a small knock. I'm not surprised it isn't heard over the loud wails. I'm getting déjà vu. This isn't the first time I've stood outside this door waiting to be heard.

The second knock causes the door to open a little wider. Deciding to commit fully to this stupid idea, I push the door open wide enough to enter the room. I figure he already hates me, so what's the worst that could happen? Once I get a look at the view inside that room, I decide it was worth any potential backlash. Even with a screaming baby, the view is spectacular.

TJ stands in front of a huge glass desk. He's shirt is off and is tucked into the back of his black gym shorts. Shorts that do nothing to hide his muscular thighs. My eyes roam over each and every muscle of his back, watching as they bunch and flex with his movements. His tattoos look like they're dancing as he moves. I'd make a fortune if I took a picture of him like this and sold it.

He's holding the baby tucked close to his chest, and I can just make out the top of its head. He's gently bouncing side to side, attempting to sooth the poor little thing. He's holding onto it like it's the most precious thing in the world, murmuring the whole time. It surprises me that this brutal looking guy can be so gentle. I've only gotten to see the hard TJ. This soft side of him is intoxicating, and I could stand here all day looking at him.

I'm lost in the sight of him, of them. So lost that I don't even notice when TJ turns and spots me standing there.

"What are you doing in here?"

Ten

TJ

Listening to Abel cry like this for the last fifteen minutes is killing me. I've made sure he's not hungry or dirty. I'm guessing it's the tooth he seems to be cutting, but the baby Tylenol he had thirty minutes ago doesn't seem to be doing shit.

Mom was supposed to have him today, but both her and dad have a sickness bug. I hoped to get most of my work done while he took his morning nap, but he's been fractious since he woke up. I can't take him home while he's this upset; there's no way I could concentrate on driving. I've tried everything I can think of to calm him, and so far nothing I try is working.

This is the part they don't mention in any of the many baby books I've read. They don't tell you what to do when you've tried *everything* to get them to stop crying. I could call my mother, but she'll just try to take over. I love her and she's been nothing but amazing with Abel, but I want to learn how to deal with this shit by myself. I can't keep running to other people for help all the time.

Shifting him in my arms, I bring his head closer to my chin, hoping he'll hear my voice over his cries. "I got you, bud. No need to cry. Your dad's got you," I keep on chatting nonsense to him, but nothing is making a difference.

I'm about to cave and call my mom when I notice movement in the reflection of the mirror to the side of my desk. Turning around, I'm surprised to see Breeze standing just inside my office. Just what I need, her to see me fail at being a dad.

"What are you doing in here?"

The words come out on a snap. It's not intentional, but having her witness this shit show is enough to set me into asshole mode.

Again.

She looks unsure of herself, shifting slightly from one foot to the other and back again, hands twisting in the bottom of her shirt.

"I heard the commotion and wanted to see if there was anything I could do to help." Her soft voice has the tiniest hint of a rasp. The sound hardly audible over the racket Abel is still making. "I've been known to work magic on my sister's babies." She shrugs and this time when she speaks, Abel's head swings in her direction. He doesn't quieten down, just looks at her as he keeps crying.

A big part of me wants to tell her *thanks, but no thanks.* That I don't need help from her or anyone else for that matter. Pride is a complex thing when you're a parent. You have to learn to accept help, even when you have a stubborn streak as wide as mine. A stubborn streak that wars with the side of me, that knows I should just accept her offer.

I have to remind myself that she's offering to help Abel, not me. My pride needs to take a back seat for once.

"You're sure?" I ask, giving her the chance to change her mind. She doesn't answer, just rolls her eyes and walks further into the room. Closer to me.

Close enough for me to smell whatever perfume it is she's wearing. It's something light and crisp, like fresh air. She doesn't touch me, but I can feel her next to me, the air between us feels charged.

Placing her hand lightly on Abel's back, Breeze rubs small circles over and over. He doesn't take his eyes off her, but the cries continue.

"Hey, handsome," she coos, a wide smile on her pretty face. "What's all this fuss about, hey?" For the first time I realize how small she is compared to me. She's barely past my shoulders.

"I think it's his teeth," I tell her. "He's not hungry, he's been changed. He hasn't missed a nap either. I have no idea what else to do for him."

"Poor little man." She pouts, rubbing her hand over his head. "Can I?" She holds her hands out toward him, looking up at me with those clear, crystal blue eyes, and I'm pretty sure I'd struggle to tell her no, no matter what she's asking of me.

"Sure." I shift the baby so she can grab ahold of him. She moves him so he's laying with his head in the crook of her arm and his body turned in toward hers. Then she starts swaying side to side.

He still doesn't stop crying, and I'm about to ask her to hand him back when Breeze does the last thing I expect.

She starts to sing.

I don't recognize the song. She's singing so low I can't make out the words, but for the first time in what feels like hours, Abel's cries slow to a few soft mewls. He brings his fist to his mouth and starts to chew on it.

"Has he had any pain relief?" she asks. Except, she doesn't just ask, she sings the question to me in the same low tone she's been using the last few minutes. Does she expect me to answer her the same way? She's shit out of luck if she does. I answer her, normally, telling her how much Tylenol he had and about the awful gel I rubbed on his gums earlier.

"Okay then, handsome, let's see what we can do for you." Making her way to the Pack'n'Play that's set up in the corner of my office, Breeze never stops swaying side to side as she goes. Of course, my eyes track every sway of her hips as she walks. Letting my gaze wander further, I take her in from head to toe. Her hair is more of a blonde than pink now, the color faded out. She's braided it and it rests over one shoulder, the other bare apart from the thin strap of her cami. I'm struck by the thought of what it might be like to run my tongue over the smooth skin that's on show. I bet she tastes fucking amazing.

Jesus fuck, there's something wrong with me.

Scrubbing my hands over my face, I follow behind her just in time to see her gently place Abel on the changing mat that rests across the top of the crib. I brace for the tears to start again, but I'm shocked as shit to see him lay there. He's perfectly content watching Breeze.

"Are these teethies bothering you?" she asks while she rubs her hands together, before she brings them to his head again. This time she runs her fingertips gently around his face, along his jaw, and around his mouth.

In all this time, neither of them have broken eye contact.

It takes a second before I realize, she's not singing anymore. Instead, she's talking to Abel, telling him what she's doing. Asking him if he likes it. Of course, he doesn't answer, but she keeps on, explaining what she's doing as she massages his tiny face.

I've never seen anything like it.

She keeps on doing this until my kid smiles at her. Fucking smiles.

She's better than a baby whisperer. She's a fucking angel. An angel who's giving me some not so angelic thoughts right now with the way she's leaning over in those yoga pants.

Add to that the fact that she's just worked a miracle on Abel? Yeah, I'm way more turned on than I should be right now. Turning to look at me, she beckons for me to come closer.

"Come watch what I'm doing," she says, still in the same low tone. "Okay, Dad, I'm not an expert, but I've done a few baby yoga classes. This typically works best if you do it every day. Don't wait for him to be in pain. Maybe make it part of his bedtime routine." She goes on to show me where to massage and how much pressure to use.

"What was with the singing?" I can't help it, I have to ask.

"Huh?" She's not paying much attention to me, instead concentrating on Abel.

"You kept singing to him, even when you were speaking to me."

"Oh." She chuckles as a pink blush steals over her face. "I read somewhere that babies don't actually understand the words we're saying, just the tone we use. You could read the Starbucks menu to him, but say it in a soothing tone, and he'll still love it." She finishes on a shrug.

"Makes sense, I suppose," I mutter, biting back the urge to tell her she could read me the damn phonebook in that voice and I'd still sit and listen to her for hours.

It's barely another minute before Abel's eyes start to droop. When he lets out a big yawn, Breeze slows down her movements, eventually tapering off when his eyes stay closed.

Definitely a miracle worker.

"Thank you," I say quietly when she takes a step away from the crib. "You didn't have to come in here and help..." I hesitate. Apologies are not my strong suit, but I owe her one "Especially after how I spoke to you earlier."

"You're probably right." I'm not shocked at her candid response. I get the feeling she isn't the type to pull any punches. "But I figured the baby wasn't the one who was a douche to me so..." Another shrug of that bare shoulder. Her words cause a smile to tip up one side of my mouth.

"Well, I apologize for earlier. Last week too. I'm not always such an ass." She doesn't answer, just eyes me speculatively before she nods.

"Okay," she says, before she moves toward the door.

"Okay?" I parrot back at her.

"Yeah, okay. You apologized. I accepted." She stops at the door, looking like she wants to say something more, but she's not sure if she should. I see the moment she decides not to say whatever is on her mind. Instead, she pulls the door open further.

"Good luck with the baby," she says on a wave. I have no idea why I say it, but it's out of my mouth before I can stop it.

"Abel. His name is Abel."

She stops then turns around slowly. When she's facing me, her warm gaze roams over me.

"Abel," she repeats. "Cute." Her smile is wide, and seeing it hits me somewhere in my chest. Why do I get the feeling she wasn't just talking about my son?

Fuck.

I'm in trouble.

Eleven

BREEZE

Why on earth did I suggest family dinner?

After an hour of listening to my older sister Ava trash talk all my life choices, I'm beyond ready to go home and eat my body weight in chocolate.

So far, she's picked holes in where I choose to live. I rent my tiny studio apartment from a lovely old lady called Mrs P; it's crazy small but cheap. According to Ava, grown women don't rent rooms above someone else's garage.

After that it was my job. Who knew being a yoga instructor wasn't a real job? I ignored the question of when I was going to pick an actual career.

As for my plans to travel? Why would I be so foolish wasting time and money traveling? Why couldn't I just vacation like normal people?

Ava fusses around the table, making sure everybody has enough food and drinks. She's in her element with everyone here to fuss over; it's what she does best. Her husband, Carl, just leaves her to it. They've been together since high school, and he's learned it's pointless to stop her when she's on a tear like this. Their ten-year-old daughter, Lainey, sits beside me, eyes glued to her iPad. Their younger two, six-year-old Jake, and Tori who is three, are in bed already.

Asa and my other brother, Beau, are also experts at tuning out Ava and her rants. We're all used to her by now.

Asa might be the oldest, but Av is only ten months younger, and when our mom passed away, she was the one to assume the parental role. She was twenty-one when it happened; Asa had just turned twenty-two. Beau and I were a lot younger, him thirteen and me just nine-years-old. She dropped out of school and put her life on hold for us. I more than appreciate everything she did for us, everything she sacrificed, but she's yet to learn how to cut the apron strings.

"As fun as it is having my life choices picked apart, I'm going to head out," I announce, standing from the table and picking up my plate of half eaten food, not bothering to look at anyone else as I go.

Scraping my leftovers into the dog's bowl, I dump my plate in the dishwasher then turn around to see Ava standing behind me.

"Which one of them sent you in to apologize?" I ask, knowing one of the guys would have pointed out how she was behaving.

"Asa." She sighs "I guess he already gave you the "act like a grown up" talk recently?"

"Yep."

"I'm sorry—"

"No, you're not, Av," I interrupt her.

"Stop being a brat," she snaps at me like I'm one of her kids, and as much as I'm willing myself to stay mad at her because she just proved my point, I can't. She's more than just my bossy big sister. She must realize herself because she deflates.

"I'm sorry. Really sorry," she says quietly.

"Me too."

"It's just that I love you and want what's best for you." She tells me something I already know.

"I know. Don't think for one second that I'm not grateful for everything you've done for me." I pull her in for a hug, wrapping my arms around her. "Mom would be so proud of you." My throat aches with the weight of the emotion that suddenly sits there. It's always the same whenever Mom gets mentioned.

"She'd be proud of us all," she says, squeezing me back.

"Well, maybe not Asa but..." I trail off when she lets out a small laugh.

"It kills me that you didn't get more time with her," Ava whispers.

"Me too," I admit, "but you always tell me I got my free spirit from her. So why does it surprise you that I want the same things she did?"

I was nine when our mom died, but she was sick for years before that. Instead of memories of day trips and activities, I have movie days and picnics in a den she'd made in her bed. Hours spent listening to her telling me to never settle. That I deserved to see the world. To take risks and live every day to the fullest.

My parents were wanderers. They married young and planned to travel the world. Asa was a welcomed surprise for them, but he hadn't made a dent in their plans. He traveled across Central America with them before his first birthday. Avalon being born a year later was the catalyst for them coming back to Savannah.

Once real life set in, the travel plans got pushed further and further back, but she never lost that wanderlust.

It didn't matter that there were more babies born, more work to do, more mundane real life. She always held out hope that one day, she'd get to see the rest of the world.

It wasn't until my dad died when I was still a baby that she realized she might never get to live those dreams.

Maybe it's because I was so young, but it was always me who hung on to every word of her stories. She would paint these vivid pictures with her words. Places she'd been, places she wanted to see.

I wanted that too.

I wanted that for me, but part of me wanted it for her too.

"I'm terrified you won't come back." Ava sniffs, gripping onto my hand.

"I'll be safe," I promise her.

"What if you meet some handsome Spanish guy and end up marrying him and have a ton of his babies? You'll be thousands of miles away, and we'll never get to see you." She cries. Ava has always had a flair for the dramatics.

I'm not sure why, but when she talks about babies and families, my mind immediately flits to TJ. To visions of him and Abel, how he held him to his chest as he cried. How perfect he looked holding him.

Yeah, my thoughts have strayed to them more than they probably should have over the last few days. I'd be lying if I said I hadn't felt drawn to him from the first time I'd seen him. That feeling has only intensified since then.

I'd also be lying if I said I hadn't been hoping to run in to TJ at work, but so far, I've yet to see him. I have so many questions. Questions I have no right to ask, but still want to know. Starting with where is the baby's mother.

I don't get to dwell on thoughts of TJ and his baby, because the rest of my family are soon bursting into the room, full of laughter and loud voices that bring me back to reality.

A reality where I have no business wondering anything about the mystery that is TJ and his adorable baby boy.

TJ

"Are you even listening to me?" My brother's voice cuts into my thoughts. No, I'm not listening to him, and that's because it's taking all of my concentration not to stare across the back yard, where the woman who's been on my mind a ridiculous amount lately, is sitting at a table with my sister-in-law and her friends.

I'd be lying if I said I wasn't hoping to run into Breeze at some point over the last few days, ever since she walked out of my office, leaving me with a hefty dose of blue balls.

I never expected to find her at my brother's house. Luckily for me, it's Poppy's baby shower, so there's a ton of people here, and I've so far managed to avoid being alone with her.

That doesn't mean she hasn't held my attention all afternoon, though. My eyes have tracked every move she's made and every person she's spoken to. I've made a point to keep my ass seated at this table with the guys, avoiding as many people as possible.

My brother's house looks like a baby shop has exploded all over it. There are pink and blue balloons everywhere, strings of lights hung in the trees.

"Sorry, what did you say?" I've not listened to a single thing anyone around me has said for the last hour.

"What the fuck is wrong with you today?"

"Nothing. Abel didn't sleep too good," I lie. He's been like a different kid since Breeze and her magic hands showed me how to calm him. He's sleeping better than ever.

"Sure," Duke scoffs. Looking around the table, I see all the guys have their eyes on me. Keir, Duke, and Hayden are all stifling a laugh.

"What's that supposed to mean?"

"It means you've been so busy staring at that chick over there for the last hour, that you haven't heard a single word we've said. Who is she anyway?" Hayden adds, leaning forward and pointing his beer bottle at the table where Breeze is sitting.

"She's nobody," I lie.

Keir look at me, eyes narrowed before he speaks. "She took over from the yoga instructor at Flex. Poppy and El have been going to her classes, and you know those two could make friends with anyone anywhere," he tells him.

"That doesn't explain why this guy has been staring at her like a creepy stalker for the last hour." Hayden nods toward me, making the rest of the guys laugh.

"I have no idea what you're talking about." Picking up my beer, I drain the last of it instead of saying anything else.

"Could have fooled me," Keir says behind his own bottle.

"I get it," Hayden continues, leaning back in his chair and crossing his arms over his chest. "She's not hard to look at. Not at all."

"You guys gossip more than the women do." Waving my empty bottle around, I stand. "Anyone want a fresh one?" I need to get out of here before I reach across the table and knock him the fuck out.

Once they've all answered, I head into the kitchen to get a few minutes peace. The guys can be real dickheads when they want to be. I'm barely in there a minute when my mom walks in.

"Where's Abel?" I ask. If her grandkids are around, Mom usually has them attached to her hip. Now that Chase is running around all over the place, it's usually my son she latches on to.

"He fell asleep, so I put him in his stroller in the shade. I just came in to make sure there's enough food left."

"There's twenty people here, Mom, and you've cooked enough for sixty."

"Well, Lucy and Scott will be here soon, and you've seen the way you boys eat. I'm surprised there's a crumb left out there."

I wait for the pang of jealously that usually comes with knowing Lucy and her boyfriend will be nearby. I'm pleasantly surprised to find I don't feel much of anything anymore. It's freeing.

Dropping a kiss on the side of my mom's head, I leave her to her fussing and head outside. The first thing I notice is that the guys are no longer sitting at the table up on the deck. They've moved down to sit where everyone else is, under an open sided tent that's been set up on the grass.

The second thing I notice is that Abel isn't in his stroller. He's being held by Breeze. I'm not going to let myself think about how right she looks holding him. Or how much I like seeing it.

Squeezing the necks of the bottles in my hand, I make my way toward the table. I'm not surprised to see that the only empty seat is next to Breeze, and I'm even less surprised to see Hayden has moved to the seat on the other side of her.

"I don't think we've met." He leans over and offers her his hand as he introduces himself. "I've not seen you around before, and I would never forget such a pretty face."

Watching him flirt with her has my teeth gritted, immediately set on edge. I accused her of flirting with Jonah at work before, but I think I knew deep down that there was nothing to that. What I was really feeling then was frustration. Frustration that I was attracted to her but couldn't do a single thing about it.

But this, this is jealousy.

Pure and simple.

A desire to stake a claim on her burns in me. One that isn't mine to stake.

A handful of conversations, the majority of which I've left looking like a jerk, and that's it. She hasn't even noticed me approach, so she's startled when I lean down and lift Abel straight out of her arms.

Settling my son on my lap, I ignore the muttering I hear coming from the direction of my family and friends. I know they're wondering what the fuck is wrong with me. Sure, I can be a dick sometimes, but being outright rude like that isn't me. Not usually anyway.

"I'm sorry," Breeze says quietly from the side of me. I don't want to look at her. I don't want to see if I've upset her again. But it's pointless trying to stop the inevitable. My gaze slides to her, and I take in her pretty features. Guilt runs through me when I see the way she shifts nervously in her seat. "He was fussing in his stroller, and everyone else was busy—"

"I've got him now. Thanks." I don't look at her before turning in my seat, effectively cutting her off.

"Spill."

"Wow. Took you a whole three minutes to follow me in here," I say to my sister-in-law without turning to face her.

As soon as I stepped into the kitchen to make a bottle for Abel, I knew at least one of those nosey fuckers would be on me.

"You try standing up from a deck chair quickly while a giant baby sits on your bladder." She huffs. "Stop avoiding and start answering. We both know that Keir will be in here any second to 'check on me'. Again." I turn to her just in time to catch the air quotes.

"He's just worried about you. We all are after what happened."

"I know," she interrupts me, knowing that I'm still not ready to talk about the shit that happened with Willow. I haven't made any peace with the whole fucked up situation, and I know my brother especially is struggling with the thought of something similar happening to his wife.

"Seriously, stop trying to distract me, and start telling me what the fuck that was out there with you and Bree." She does an excited little jump and claps her hands together.

Fuck me.

"Nothing to tell, sis." I busy myself with the formula and water in front of me. Hoping like hell she'll drop it but knowing she's like a rabid dog with this shit.

"So let me get this straight," she starts. "You've been staring at her all afternoon, then you snap at her for no reason. That's classic schoolyard boy with crush behavior, you know."

"Whatever you say, Pop," I scoff, aiming for dismissive but probably failing miserably.

"She's very pretty."

"She is. She's also very *young*," I remind her, because as beautiful as Breeze is, she's a hell of a lot younger than me. With a lot less baggage.

"Stop looking for excuses!" Poppy exclaims, rolling her eyes at me. "You should ask her out."

"I don't need to look for an excuse, Pop. I need to concentrate on Abel and work. I don't have room in my life for anything else." And for once, a part of me wishes that wasn't the case.

I've always pushed women away, used excuses to avoid commitment. When I was still fighting, I used training as an excuse. When that ended, it was work, the gym, and how busy that kept me.

Hell, I was sure I was in love with Lucy for a while, and I still couldn't commit. I can't help but think that if anyone could change that it's Breeze. She's intrigued me from the very first time I saw her.

"You can have a life too. You *deserve* a life too."

Wrapping Poppy up in hug, I kiss the top of her head before answering.

"I'm not saying that one day I won't find someone, but right now the timing is shitty. Things are about to get crazy with Jonah's training schedule. I'm barely going to have time for Abel, let alone a woman. I mean this in the best possible way, but I don't need the distraction right now. And anyway, I'm pretty sure she hates me."

And if she doesn't hate me already, she should.

"Well if you aren't going to ask her out, you could at least offer her a ride home."

"Why would I do that?"

"Because it's the least you could do after being an ass to her earlier. And she rode her bicycle here, and I'm pretty sure she has a flat tire."

She wouldn't do that, would she?

"Really? You took the air out of her tires? That's crazy, even for you," I groan.

"*I* did no such thing," she says, a smirk lighting up her face.

"I have no idea how my brother puts up with you." She laughs off my comments before turning and flouncing back out to the yard.

An hour later and of course I'm giving Breeze a ride home. I kept my mouth shut when she discovered the flat tire, not willing to give into Poppy's game. And I was doing fucking great at ignoring the bullshit until Hayden stepped up and offered her a ride home.

Of course that fucker did.

I'd had the bike in the back of my truck and Breeze in the front seat before I could think twice about what I was doing.

Now, the silence surrounding us is thick. Abel is asleep in the back, so we don't even have him to distract us from it.

Turning on the radio, I flick through the channels, trying to find something to cut through the awkwardness.

She never even looks my way, and I know she doesn't because my eyes are on her more than they should be for someone who's driving.

Seeing her sitting there, head against the glass, shoulders slumped, I know I should clear the air between us. But how do I do that, when I'm not exactly sure why I'm unable to act like a grown up around her?

"Thanks for this." I turn toward her when she speaks, but she's still concentrating hard on the scenery flying past the glass.

"No problem," I say, running my hand over my jaw, unsure of how to proceed with this, but knowing I should. "I'm sorry I was a dick."

"Which time?" she says without missing a beat.

"I guess I deserve that." I wince at her come back.

"All of them?" I keep my eyes on the road as I wait for her to answer, but she doesn't. I decide to keep on anyway.

"I should have said thank you for helping with Abel that day. I've been doing the stuff you showed me, and he's been so much happier."

"Really? That's amazing." Risking a glance her way, I see the tiniest of smiles pull up the corner of her mouth. Makes a change from the scowl she usually ends up wearing around me.

With the air cleared, we actually manage to hold a conversation for the rest of the way to her place, and when we pull up outside of a small two-story house that's just a few blocks away from mine, I'm almost tempted to keep driving. I'm not ready to say goodbye to her.

"If you open the garage, I'll take the bike inside for you," I tell her, turning the engine off.

"Oh that's okay, the garage isn't mine, just the apartment above it."

Looking toward where she's pointing, I see a set of metal steps that lead up to what must be the smallest apartment above the tiny garage.

"You live up there? Alone?" I ask stupidly because she's already told me she does. "Is that safe?" The thought of her up there alone fills me with dread.

"Wow, you almost sound like you care." Taking her seatbelt off, she hops out of the truck. "Careful, I might start thinking you like me."

"The door looks like it's made of cardboard for fuck sake," I say, following her.

"I'm fine. The apartment is fine." She stands at the back of the truck, waiting for me to get the bike for her, arms crossed over her chest.

"Do you have a repair kit for this thing?"

"I'll find one."

"What time are you due at Flex tomorrow?" I ask, watching as her brow crinkles in confusion.

"Nine a.m. Why?"

"Leave the bike with me tonight, and I'll pick you up around eight thirty in the morning."

"What?!" The look of shock on her face is almost comical. I don't give her a chance to argue. I'm back in my truck and driving away before she can say another word, pleased as fuck I've found a way to spend a bit more time with her tomorrow.

BREEZE

Pacing back and forth in front of the living room window, I check again to see if TJ is here yet. How the hell did I get into this situation? One minute he's acting like he hates me, the next he's bending over backward to be helpful. I'm getting whiplash from the back and forth with him.

Never for one minute did I think it would be so awkward seeing him yesterday, but the look on his face when he saw me sitting there knocked me back. Heat fills my cheeks at the memory of him taking Abel out of my arms the way he did. I only held him because Poppy asked me too.

The sound of a car pulling up outside stops my thoughts from wandering too much. My stomach dips when I see TJ getting out of his truck. Why does he have to be so good looking? It would be much easier to stay mad at him if he was ugly.

I don't move as he opens the door to the truck and climbs out. I'm too busy staring at the tight athletic shirt he has on. The way it molds to his arms is mesmerizing. Being stuck in such close proximity to him for the next twenty minutes is going to suck.

Gathering my bag and a jacket, I open the door just before he can knock. I'm keen to get this over with. Taking a deep breath and painting on a fake smile, I meet him just as he hits the top of the rickety stairs outside of my front door.

"Morning," he says, and for a second, I get a flash in my mind of what it might be like to have that deep voice greet me every single morning. Heat suffuses my cheeks, and all I can do is smile in return. He shifts to the side, letting me walk down first. The space is so narrow I have no choice but to brush past him, and the briefest touch of his skin on mine sends goose bumps skittering all over me.

Opening the back door to put my bags in, I'm surprised to see Abel in his car seat. "Hey, little guy," I coo, running my finger over his hand. I get a wet smile and a finger grab in return.

"He's coming to work with me for the morning; my mom will be in to get him later," TJ tells me once we're on the road.

"It must be difficult, juggling work and a baby on your own?" I realize too late that it sounds like I'm fishing for information. Luckily TJ doesn't seem fazed by the question.

"It is. But I'm lucky, my family is amazingly supportive, and he's pretty chilled as far as babies go," he says, pride evident in his tone and in the smile on his face when he talks about his son.

"Well I don't know you very well, but from what I've seen you're doing a great job."

His eyes don't leave the road, so I take the opportunity to look at him uninterrupted for a minute. Taking in the dark, slightly too long hair that I could see myself sliding my fingers through, to the dark stubble that covers what I know is a strong jaw. Because I'm studying him, I see the bob of his tanned throat as he swallows before speaking.

"Thank you." It's barely a murmur, but I hear him. I hear how he hates taking a compliment, but I also hear he's proud to be told he's doing good.

Taking a deep breath, I need to snap myself out of this trance he seems to put me in. Even when he's being a dick to me, I'm drawn to him. TJ being nice is lethal. I don't know that I can survive the nice version of him.

"Did you manage to fix the bike?" I go for a change of topic, thinking we both could use it right now.

"Well there was no puncture, so I just pumped some air into it. It seems to be holding okay, though."

"No puncture?" I question, because that wheel was flat as a pancake. I can't see how it would be like that without a hole in it of some sort. TJ shifts uncomfortably in his seat, and the knuckles on the hand that's resting on the gear stick whiten.

"Yep. I double checked. No puncture."

"That's good. I have to ride over to my second job later today, and I'll never make it if I have to walk." I'm grateful that he's saved me the hassle of trying to get a new tire.

"You have a second job?" His eyes turn to me briefly.

"Well, technically it's not an official second job. My best friend owns a coffee shop, and I help her out from time to time. And it works out well because I'm only at Flex part time. She's taking on staff this week, so this will be my last shift working for her," I ramble. TJ doesn't seem to mind, though. I know he's concentrating on the road, but it feels like he's interested in what I'm saying.

"Will you be looking for another job now then? Something full time?" Again, his dark eyes risk a glance at me.

"Maybe, if something comes up. I'm saving to go traveling soon, so I'll take all the work I can get."

"Traveling, huh?"

"Yeah, once my time at Flex is done, I'll be heading off to Europe."

This time his eyes are surprised when he looks my way. "No shit?"

"You shouldn't swear when baby ears are so close," I tell him, cringing when I realize, I sound just like Ava. TJ doesn't seem to hear me, though. He looks back at the road and drives the rest of the way in silence, seemingly lost in his thoughts.

Later that evening, I'm cleaning up after my last class of the day, and I'm beat. With all of the equipment packed away, I'm ready to go home and crawl into bed for a few hours. I got hardly any sleep last night, the events of the baby shower playing on a loop front and center in my mind all night. Between that and riding back and forth to Deja Brew this afternoon, I'm dead on my feet.

Flicking the last of the studio lights off, I lock up and zip the key away in my bag. I'm almost to the front door when I hear my name being called. Turning around I see a very sweaty TJ jogging my way. Fresh TJ looked good this morning; sweaty TJ right now is doing wonderful things for my imagination. Except, I'm now imagining him being sweaty for reasons other than a work out.

"Hey, I'm glad I caught you. I was going to come by your place on my way home."

"My place?" I ask, gripping my backpack hard to stop myself from reaching out and touching a bead of sweat that just dropped off the end his hair.

"I have an idea I'd like to run past you," he says, indicating toward the empty reception desk and the seats behind it. I have no idea what he could want to discuss with me, but I follow behind him to sit.

"I was thinking about what you were saying earlier, about getting another job, and I was thinking maybe you'd consider working for me?"

"I already work with you," I reply, completely confused.

"No, you work for Flex," he laughs. "I want you to work for me, watching Abel."

"But I'm not a nanny."

"I don't need a nanny for him. I need someone here, at work, to take care of him when I have to be in the ring with Jonah, or in meetings, that kind of thing. Pop and my mom are doing it now, but with Chase and the new baby coming so soon, I'd like to take some of the pressure off them." He sighs deeply before he speaks again. "I'm not going to go into detail, but Abel and I, we had a rough start. I want him to be around as much as possible; it's good for both of us. I can only do that if he's here. I have too much on my plate right now, but I can't drop Jonah. It's not fair to him either."

I'm beyond shocked at his request. After the encounters we've had so far, I was pretty sure he hated me. This is the very last thing I would have expected him to ask. And I'm more than a bit gutted that I have to turn him down.

"I have a timetable here that isn't flexible, so I can't offer you that much time."

The smile he flashes my way is obviously the one he uses to get whatever he wants, and I swear I see a dimple come out to play too.

"One of the perks of owning this place is that *my* schedule can be flexible. I'll work around you as much as I can, and anything we can't do between us, we'll work out as it happens.

"TJ..." I trail off when I can't find the words to tell him no.

"Please? Abel obviously likes you. You're good with him, and you won't have to look for a second job. I'll make other arrangements by the time you leave for Europe."

It's on the top of my tongue.

'Sorry, I can't.'

I want to say the words.

I'm about to say the words.

He must see it in my face because he lets out a deep breath, and his shoulders droop.

I'm not sure which of us is more surprised when I do finally speak.

"Okay. I'll help you"

"You did what?" Fleur shouts at me, spraying the mouthful of wine she just drank all over the table we're sat at.

"I know!" I groan, letting my head drop onto my arms where they rest on the table in front of me. "I'm an idiot."

"You're not an idiot," she says, not even trying to hide the laughter in her voice.

Instead of going home to bed like I'd planned, I came straight to my best friend. We've been sitting on her tiny roof terrace, the bottle of wine between us almost all gone. I've told her all about TJ and my new job helping him with Abel.

"Only an idiot would let a guy speak to her like shit, *repeatedly*, then cave the first time he asked a favor. Damn that stupid dimple." I throw back the last of my wine before thrusting my empty glass at Fleur for her to refill.

"A dimple? If he's as hot as you say he is, and he has a dimple, you were doomed from the beginning, girl. Don't beat yourself up over it."

"He's stupidly hot. He's make dumb decisions kinda hot."

"What did you say his last name is?" she asks, pulling out her phone.

"Harmon, why?" The wine must be hitting me because it's not until it's too late that I realize she's looking him up on the Internet. "What are you doing?" I try to grab the phone out of her hand, but she's expecting it and moves before I can reach her.

"You weren't lying, girl, he is hot as fuck." She tells me something I already know.

"Let me see." I wedge myself into the chair next to her so I can see the screen with her. She has his Facebook profile up, and it's open for everyone to see. "He's not on here much. It's mostly shared stuff about the gym. Let's skip to his photos" I should stop her, there's something creepy about it, but I can't seem to bring myself to do it.

I want to know more about him. He's a closed book that is begging to be read.

"Is that the baby?" She tilts the screen my way showing me a picture of a shirtless TJ holding a tiny baby on his chest. It's the same view I got in his office last week, but Abel is much smaller in the picture, his head covered in dark hair resting on TJ's shoulder.

"Is this Abel's mom?" She stops on a picture of Poppy, holding Abel.

"No. I don't think there are any of her on there." It hits me that there were pictures of Abel and the rest of TJ's family all over his office, the same at his brother's house, but not a single one of anyone who could be Abel's mom. I know it's not appropriate, I should wait for him to tell me what happened to her, but I can't stop myself from doing what I'm about to do.

"Keep looking," I urge. As she scrolls through, I don't see any pregnant women in any of the pictures. She's going further and further back when I notice more and more pictures of TJ and Lucy. I've met her at the gym a few times, and she was at Poppy's baby shower, but I've never seen Lucy and TJ speak to each other. Judging by how close they are in most of these, and the way he's looking at her, they've had some kind of relationship.

"Is she his girlfriend?" Fleur asks quietly.

"No. She works at the gym, and she has a boyfriend. He was at the baby shower with her."

Even knowing that she isn't with TJ, I can't help the burst of jealousy I feel when I see the connection they shared. It's palpable through the tiny screen and grainy images in front of me.

I let Fleur snoop, hoping to get answers to some of the questions I've not been able to get out of my head. Instead, I've just ended up with a ton more.

TJ

Throwing down the crappy cards Hayden just dealt, I tag the bottle of beer off the table in front of me, downing half of it in a few gulps.

"I'm out."

The guys are over for poker night, and so far, they've spent more time digging in to me over Breeze than actually playing cards.

"Let me get this right." Hayden throws a couple more chips onto the pile building up in the center of the table. "You go all caveman on her ass and practically drag her into your truck, then instead of asking her out—you know, like a normal person—you offer her a job? What the fuck is wrong with you?"

"I told you. I don't see her like that." I sigh.

"Liar." Duke coughs, making the others laugh.

"Laugh all you like, assholes."

"You sure having her work for you is a good idea?" Keir asks, throwing down his cards.

"Why not? She's good with Abel, and it takes the pressure off Mom for a while. Makes sense to me." I shrug.

"And you think you'll be able to keep your hands off her, spending so much time with her?"

"I'm not a teenager. I can control my dick, you know. And anyway, she's not my type," I tell him, starting to get pissed at this conversation. "Remind me again, why I invited you all over here?"

"You might not be a teenager, but you looked like you were struggling not to act like one at the baby shower," Duke says. He's the quiet one of the group, only speaking when he really has something to say. "I thought you were about to push her over like you were in the yard at school or something," he adds, throwing his cards down on the table.

"I don't know what you guys were seeing, but you're wrong. Can we change the subject now?" I huff.

"Like you can speak," Keir laughs at Duke. "I distinctly remember someone else acting like a lovesick fool at Pop's first baby shower." Duke's face splits with a shit-eating grin before he speaks.

"Yeah"—he smirks—"that was a good day."

"Dude, El is like a sister to me. I don't even wanna know what has that smile on your face." I feel my lip curl in disgust. Looking over at Keir, I see he's wearing a similar expression.

"Welcome to my life, except Poppy actually is my sister, and I have to see that look on his face every damn time I see him." Duke points at Keir who just grins back.

"Serious talk for a minute," my brother says when the chuckles die down. "There's no reason why you couldn't pursue something with Breeze if you wanted to. She seems like a nice girl..."

"How can I go there again? With anyone? You saw the mess I was in after the whole Lucy fiasco. I can't check out like that now that I have Abel. It's not an option." I hope my tone leaves no room for argument. I'm over this whole discussion.

"You think you're the first guy to turn stupid over a woman?" Hayden asks.

"I sure as fuck did," Keir mutters, obviously remembering the time when his life went off the rails after Poppy left him.

"Made my fair share of mistakes with El too, before I pulled my head outta my ass," Duke chimes in.

"See, learn from their mistakes. Stay single." Hayden holds out his hand for a high five.

"You're an idiot," I say before leaving the table to grab some more chips and to check Abel on the monitor. He's back to sleeping through the night for the most part, but I keep the video monitor on anyway.

I get back to the table just in time to see Hayden scoop the poker chips from the center toward his side of the table.

"You guys are making this too easy tonight," he gloats.

"I'm fucking beat," Duke says, scrubbing his hands down his bearded face. "Jude is hardly sleeping. The twins are a cakewalk compared to him lately." Duke and Elliott's baby boy was born the same day as Abel. I was on my way to see them when Jessie saw me in the hospital hall that day. If I hadn't been there, I might have never known Abel existed.

"I'm not looking forward to those days again." Keir sighs. "Speaking of screaming babies, how's Abel sleeping now?" my brother asks.

"Good. Better." I shift in my seat, hoping he doesn't press for details.

"What's the secret? I need all the help I can get." Duke leans closer, rapt attention on me, like I have the secret to world peace and I'm about to share it.

"Actually, we're doing some baby massage stuff before bed." I shrug like baby massage is an everyday thing.

"What the fuck is that?" Hayden asks, confusion on his face.

"Exactly what I said. He gets a bath before bed, then he lays on his mat while I do some massage and stretches with him. He goes out like a light after that."

"So it's like yoga? For babies?" Keir smirks. "I wonder where you could have possibly learned that? A certain pink-haired yoga instructor, maybe?"

Rolling my eyes, I grab the deck of cards, ignoring the cackles of laughter around me.

"Yuck it up, assholes." I deal the cards. "Yes, Breeze showed me a few things," I admit reluctantly.

"I wouldn't say no to her showing me a few things either," Hayden mutters.

"She's off limits," I spit the words out, wishing that I could take them back almost immediately when I see Hayden's face light up.

"Off limits? Why would she be off limits?" he asks.

"I'm done discussing this with you; are we playing poker or not?" I try to deflect once again.

Thankfully they give me a break, and all talk of Breeze stops. I know they don't mean it, but the more she's brought up, the more fucking confused I feel.

And that confusion sticks with me for the rest of the night. Even after the guys are gone, my mind whirls with thoughts of her. I meant it when I told Keir that I'd be able to keep my hands off her. I've had enough self-discipline for that.

The problem is, I'm finding it harder and harder to remember why I have to keep my hands off her.

The next day I'm still distracted. Instead of focusing on the computer screen in front of me, I find my eyes keep wandering to the clock. Breeze is due down here to sit with Abel soon. My aim for today is to not be a dick to her.

The door is pushed open, and I feel myself deflate when I see it's not Bree. It's Lucy.

"Hey," she says, taking the seat opposite me. "I have that revised schedule you wanted."

She hands me a few pieces of paper before turning to make a fuss of Abel where he's sitting in a bouncer next to me.

I scan over the changes I asked her to help me make. Changes that mean I have a reason to see Breeze more often.

"There's a few late sessions on here, was Jonah okay with that? Can he start tonight?"

"He was fine with it. He's desperate to get in that ring. You've done an amazing job with him, TJ." One of the things that had first attracted me to Lucy was how much she loved Flex and what we do here. It might have been me and Keir to get Flex up and running, but I don't know if we'd be half as successful if it wasn't for Lucy. She's here more than we are these days.

"Thanks, Luce."

"No problem. How's this gorgeous boy been doing?" She coos at him, causing him to kick his little legs in excitement. My kid is such a flirt.

"He's good," I tell her, but she's too busy making faces at the baby to care about what I said.

"Alright. I gotta get back to work." She stands and makes her way to the door. "Don't forget we have that budget meeting tomorrow too," she says, making me groan. I hate that side of owning a business.

"Do I have to be there? You and Keir make all the decisions anyway." I sulk.

"Stop being a baby," she laughs. "I'll bring the coffee and donuts; you just have to show up with the company check book."

"Alright, alright." I sigh. "I'll see you in the morning."

"It's a date," she says, laughing to herself as she goes.

BREEZE

When I agreed to help look after Abel, the last thing I thought I'd be doing was babysitting so that TJ could go on a fucking date.

"It's a date."

I felt like such an idiot, standing outside of TJ's office about to knock on the door when Lucy walked out. My stomach dropped at the last words she said before leaving. TJ didn't even have the decency to look embarrassed; he'd just straight up asked me to watch Abel for him.

My legs peddle furiously, pumped by the anger that's coursing through me. I'm angry at myself for being stupid enough to be attracted to him. I'm livid with myself because I was starting to think he felt something for me too.

I refuse to believe that I'm the only one who feels the chemistry that zips between us every time we're near one another. No, he's attracted to me just as much as I'm attracted to him. The difference is he's ignoring it and taking someone else out on a date. Someone he has a past with.

I should cancel, leave him to find someone else to watch Abel. I wish I was the kind of person who could do that and not die from the guilt. No, I'll go and watch him. Smile when TJ leaves, then I'll eat my feelings away.

By the time I've chained the bike up at the side of TJ's house, I'm a sweaty mess.

Fantastic. I'm sure he'll regret his choice not to date me when he catches sight of me like this.

This is the first time I've been to his house, and I'm pleasantly surprised to see how neat it is. His neighborhood is relatively new, but his house looks older than the rest. Set back slightly from the road and surrounded by trees. I can easily imagine sitting on the wide wrap-around porch. He really should get a swing out here.

I don't make it to the front door before it swings open. My heart beats faster at the sight of TJ standing there, Abel perched on his hip. I'm surprised to see he's not changed since I saw him a few hours ago at work. He's in yet another tight-fitting T-shirt and running shorts, those glorious leg muscles on full display.

Thankfully, Abel squeals when he sees me, breaking me out of my greedy staring session.

"Hey," I say on a somewhat false smile that soon fades when I see the serious look on TJ's face.

"How did you get here?" he barks without so much as a hello first.

"Nice to see you too. Why yes, I would love to come inside." My sarcastic side decides to show up.

"Don't be a smartass"

"Don't be an ass. Period," is my not so mature response. "I rode the bike."

"I would have picked you up," he says, shifting to the side slightly, allowing me to walk into the open hallway. This place is stunning. It's obviously just been renovated, everything is immaculate. My eyes work to take everything in as TJ walks toward the back of the house.

"I'm only a few blocks away, it's good exercise."

"Bree, you work out all day long. It's your job." *Bree.* I can't stop the shiver I get down my spine when he says my name. A nickname that my mother used to call me. He seems just as shocked as me that it slipped out, and a faint blush lights his cheeks. The air in the room heats, and neither of us seem keen to break the moment. His gaze drops from my eyes, over my heated cheeks, and finally landing on my lips. Is he thinking about kissing me the same way I'm thinking about kissing him?

The moment is shattered when the ringing of a cell phone sounds from the side table I'm standing next to. Looking down I see the one thing I need to remind me that this man is off limits.

Lucy calling.

That's all it takes.

TJ exhales a deep breath before he silences the call. "Come through to the kitchen. I've written down everything you need to know."

The dismissal stings. Yes, I'll definitely be eating my feelings later when Abel goes to bed.

Once TJ has shown me where everything is and explained Abel's schedule, I take the baby from his arms expecting TJ to go get changed. Instead, he grabs a backpack from next to the door and a bunch of keys.

"I shouldn't be too long. If there's any issues at all, anything you need, call me." He smooths his hand over Abel's head just before bending to drop a kiss there too. I can easily imagine him moving to kiss me next. Of course, he doesn't. He offers me a small smile before turning to leave.

Since he was already bathed and in his pajamas, Abel and I have spent the evening playing with his toys. Now it's his bedtime, and I'm in a beautiful wooden rocking chair that's set up in the corner of his nursery.

The walls are a soft sage green, there's a beautiful hand-painted tree taking up the whole wall behind the crib, and dotted amongst the branches are photographs in all different shapes and sizes.

I recognize Poppy, Keir, and Chase in a few of them. There's a collage frame with four different images, all of the same older couple holding who I assume is a tiny Abel. There's no doubt these are TJ's parents, even if I hadn't met them at the baby shower, I'd recognize them. TJ and Keir take after their dad. He's just an older version of them. His mother looks thrilled to be holding her grandson, and the pure joy on her face causes my chest to ache. My mom missed that. Ava had her first baby just a few years after mom died; she would have loved being a grandma. The last picture is slightly larger than the others. It's held my attention since the second I sat in this chair thirty minutes ago. A shirtless TJ is holding a newborn Abel against his chest, wires trailing from his tiny body. His head is angled down looking at his son, but you can still see the mix of fear and wonder on TJ's face. This family has been through so much, and seeing this picture causes my heart to squeeze.

The absence of any pictures of Abel with his mom is stark, but after stalking TJ's social media it's not at all surprising.

Once Abel's eyes start to droop, I move him to his crib, laying him down and covering him with the soft blanket that's draped over the end. According to TJ, he self-settles easily. As tempting as it is to keep a hold of him until he's asleep, I understand that TJ needs me to keep to Abel's routine as much as possible. He has been so well behaved all night, but even so, it hasn't been easy. He needs a grown up for everything. TJ is doing this alone. I was already intrigued by the man, but I now have a deeper respect for him.

It's almost ten-thirty, and I've eaten more pizza and ice cream than should be legal, but it hasn't stopped my mind from wandering to thoughts of TJ and his date. Not even Dirty Dancing on the huge flat screen TV in TJ's man cave is helping. I'm about to call Fleur just for a distraction when I hear a key turning in the front door. I can't see it from here, and I'm suddenly terrified that he might not be alone.

Oh God!

What do I do if he brought her back here? I'm standing and straightening my clothes and hair when an exhausted looking TJ walks into the room. Dropping his bag, he moves further into the room.

"How has he been?"

"He was perfect. He ate and slept on schedule. He's been asleep since eight-ish," I tell him.

"Good. I can't thank you enough for tonight. Did you eat? I didn't think to make sure there was food here before I left, sorry." He surprises me by collapsing onto the sofa. I expected him to show me to the door.

"I ordered a pizza; there's plenty left if you want some?" I offer.

"Sit. Let me go grab some. Want a beer or anything?" he asks. But I'm too confused to answer. He comes back into the room, pizza box balanced on one hand, two beer bottles and two waters on top, and I'm still standing there, unsure of what to do.

"Do you have somewhere you need to be?" he asks when he sees me standing in the same spot he left me in.

"No, I just thought..."

"Sit," he repeats, patting the sofa next to him. I know I should probably just go, but I never claimed to be sensible.

Snagging one of the waters, I take a seat a little further down the sectional.

"What are we watching?" TJ asks.

"You don't know what this is?" I point at the screen where Patrick Swayze is in a lake, lifting Jennifer Grey above his head.

"No. Should I?"

"Dirty Dancing is a classic!" I exclaim, hand over my heart in mock shock. "It's one of the best love stories ever told."

"If you say so. I've never seen it." He laughs at me.

"Let me guess, you're more of an action movie kinda guy? I bet Fast and Furious is your favorite?"

TJ leans toward me ever so slightly before he answers. His words hitting me in really—really—inappropriate places.

"There's nothing wrong with Fast and Furious occasionally." The smirk on his face makes it obvious he's not talking movies anymore, and I feel a deep red blush creep over my cheeks. He's not acting like a man who's just been on a date with another woman. Then again, he's shown on more than one occasion he can be a dick, so maybe this is normal behavior for him.

Instead of answering, I roll my eyes and turn back toward the screen, ignoring the small chuckle that comes from TJ. I keep my eyes on the movie as he finishes eating, but once he's done, I start to feel a little awkward, unsure why I'm here still.

"How was your night anyway?" I break the silence, but really wanting to ask him where he's been, even knowing that's not an option.

"Good. The schedule we have Jonah on is a little crazy, but it's always like this when a fight is on the cards."

He's been with Jonah? Had I been jumping to conclusions when I assumed he was going out with Lucy?

Shit.

"You've been training?" I ask, like the idiot I obviously am.

"Where did you think I was?" he asks, confusion on his handsome face.

"Well, when I was outside your office you and Lucy were making plans, so I assumed..." I trail off, not wanting to finish the sentence. He stares at me a beat before his head drops back on the sofa, and he lets out a loud laugh.

"I know I haven't always been the nicest to you, but even I wouldn't ask you to watch my son while I was out on a date." His hand reaches toward mine where it rests between us, but I'm far enough away that just the tips of his fingers graze over the back of my hand. The touch is barely there, but I feel it everywhere. My eyes fly up to meet his. He swallows once before dropping his eyes to his hands. He leaves his fingers on me for a few more seconds before he pulls away.

"I should go," I say quietly.

"No. You are not riding that bike at this time of night. I don't care how close your place is, and I can't wake Abel up to drive you."

"I'll just call an Uber."

"Just stay. I'll take you home in the morning before work." I should tell him no thanks. I should go home and put some distance between us.

Instead, I find myself caving once again. My willpower crumbles around this man.

Before I know it, I'm being shown to a small bedroom that's opposite TJ's room. He leaves me alone for a minute before returning with something clutched in his hand.

"Here's something for you to sleep in." He places the small bundle of fabric on the bed.

"Thanks." I want to say something more, anything that would start a conversation so he'll stay and talk for a while longer. After a beat of silence, he turns to leave, stopping in the doorway and turning back to me.

"Thanks for watching Abel tonight. It was a weight off my mind knowing he was here with you. You're great with him." He doesn't give me the chance to respond before he leaves the room, closing the door as he goes.

BREEZE

Trying to sleep is a waste of time.

I've been tossing and turning for the last two hours. Trying to sleep with TJ's scent all over this shirt of his I'm wearing is like torture. Throwing the heavy blankets off my legs, I pull my socks on so I can go downstairs to make a warm drink. Hopefully this will help me finally get some sleep.

Pulling the door open, I quietly make my way downstairs. Once I'm in the kitchen, I warm some milk to make cocoa. Taking the throw off the back of the sofa, I curl up in the chair next to the large French doors at the back of the kitchen. It's too dark to see much of anything out there, the view of the lake that I caught earlier swallowed up by the dark. Right now, I can only see the stars in the inky sky. Opening the Kindle app on my phone, I try my best to get lost in the story on the screen.

It's no use, my mind is stuck on thoughts of TJ. He's in this house, so close to where I'm sitting. My mind won't stop conjuring images of him in bed, how he looks while he sleeps. I'm so lost in these thoughts I don't notice TJ has walked into the room until he's right next to me.

"Couldn't sleep either?" His voice cuts through the quiet night, making me jump in my seat.

"TJ! You scared the crap out of me!" My voice comes out an octave higher than normal.

"I spoke to you when I came in here, but you must have been so lost in thought that you didn't hear me. I thought you might have been sleeping." He chuckles. I move my eyes back to the doors, as if he might somehow be able to work out just what, or who, my thoughts have been on.

"Why are you up?" I ask but don't get a response.

"Stuff on my mind, I guess." He sighs eventually, obviously not wanting to talk about it.

"I bet you get great views here in the summer," I say, attempting to distract him from whatever is on his mind.

"I think so, we only moved in a few months ago." Turning to face him, I see his gaze trained out the window. "I was in an apartment before Abel came along, but I wanted him to have a yard to eventually run around in."

It's on the tip of my tongue to ask questions, but I know it's not my place. Instead, I keep quiet. TJ runs hot and cold with me, and I never know which version of him I'll be getting. The last thing I want is to ask him something that will have him shutting down on me again. No, it's safer to keep my questions to myself.

"It couldn't have been much fun, moving with a tiny baby."

"I'm lucky to have my family. I'd be lost trying to do this parenting stuff on my own." He chuckles.

"What happened to her? Abel's mom?" So much for keeping my questions to myself. Luckily, TJ doesn't seem offended by my asking.

"You mean you haven't heard the gossip at work?" he says on a laugh, one that's devoid of any humor.

"Gossip isn't my thing," I tell him honestly. "You don't have to tell me. I know it's none of my business." I assume the conversation is over when he doesn't answer for a few minutes. He's still staring out of the glass doors, seemingly lost in his thoughts, so I take full advantage and let my gaze rest on his face for a while. Even in profile, in the dark, he's easily the most handsome man I've ever seen.

"She died." It's a whisper, but the weight of it fills the room. Even though I assumed that something like this had happened, it still stings to see the sadness on his face.

"I'm sorry." I know that he's probably heard it a million times, but what else can I say? I'd pretty much come to this conclusion on my own anyway, but it still fills me with a sadness to know that Abel will never get to grow up with his mom. I know how that feels all too well.

Reaching over I squeeze his hand. He looks at me, and I'm taken aback by the sadness on his face. Offering me a small smile, he flips his hand over and threads his fingers through mine. The action causes my breath to catch. He's lost in thought, and I'm sure he doesn't even notice he's done it. I want to revel in how right his hand feels entwined with mine, but instead he speaks again.

"Thank you. Actually, we weren't together. Abel is the result of a bottle of Jack and some poor decisions." I get the feeling he struggles with talking about anything related to Abel's mom.

"I'm still sorry. For both of you," I tell him. "Both my parents died when I was a child, so I can relate a little." TJ's hand convulses in mine.

"That must have been rough. How old were you?"

"I wasn't even a year old when my dad passed. He had a massive heart attack while at work one day. I have no memories of him, but my mom used to say my eldest brother was dad born again so I have an idea of what he was like at least," I chuckle. "She loved him until she died, and she made sure we all grew up knowing how much he loved us."

"And your mom?" he asks quietly, and now it's my turn to keep my gaze trained on the night pressing in against the glass we're still sat in front of.

"She was amazing. She was diagnosed with cancer the when I was around five-years-old. She fought so hard, and she won that first time. The second time it was rampant through her whole body before she even suspected. She died when I was nine. My sister came home from college and took over raising us younger kids."

"You're amazing." Meeting his eyes, I let the compliment wash over me. "You've been through all that, and you're still one of the brightest people I've ever met."

"I learned that life is short, TJ. My mom would always make me promise that I'd live it to the fullest, every single day. She fought her battle for years; I figured the least I could do to honor her was live how she wanted me to." I shrug.

"That's a beautiful way to look at it." The smile he sends my way is devastating. I need to get out of here before I do something stupid, like lean over and kiss him. I start to pull my hand from his so I can stand up, but he squeezes my fingers, causing me to stop and look at him.

"Thanks again. For tonight." I get the feeling he doesn't mean just watching his son.

"Anytime. Now come on, bedtime. We'll both be useless tomorrow if we don't get some sleep." I pull him up so he's standing in front of me. My hand drops from his, and I feel the loss immediately.

Once we're standing in the hallway outside the room I'm sleeping in, I expect TJ to keep walking, but he stops right behind me, close enough for me to feel the heat of his breath on my neck. Turning around to face him, I expect him to take a step back, but he stays locked in place. He's so tall compared to me that I'm looking at his throat when I feel his fingers gently stroke under my chin, tilting my head back so he can look me in the eye.

"Breeze." He breathes my name, and I don't just hear it—I feel it. My name has never been said like that before, by anyone. Like it hurts him to say it, but in the best possible way.

My mouth dries with nerves because I'm certain he's about to kiss me. I'm half thrilled at the thought of it, half terrified. The fingers that were just under my chin shift to cup my jaw, before he cups the back of my head oh so gently.

I'm a split second away from begging him to kiss me.

The air around us seems to be on pause. It's a timeless vacuum that could be mere seconds or hours or days.

But I don't have to beg because he leans in the last inch needed for our lips to meet. His mouth strokes over mine softly, like he's learning the dip of my lips.

The kiss is slow and soft and so *right*.

It's also over way too quickly.

"Goodnight, beautiful Bree," he whispers against my mouth and before I know it, I'm standing alone in the hallway, fingers pressed to my lips, wondering what the hell just happened.

Seventeen

TJ

I knew that it would be a mistake to kiss her, but it was pointless fighting the inevitable.

It was just a matter of time before it happened. Especially after seeing her sitting in my house, wearing my shirt, looking like she was meant to be right there. I'm not sure I've ever felt so comfortable with a woman before, comfortable enough to almost tell her the truth about Willow and all the mistakes I've made. The only reason I stopped short of spilling the whole sorry tale was the fact that I was sure she'd be disgusted with me if she knew the truth.

No. I'll keep that to myself if there's even the slightest chance that Breeze will look at me differently.

I've quickly become addicted to being around her.

Now I have to work out what the fuck to do about it.

After spending the rest of the night staring at the ceiling, I finally gave up trying to sleep around the time the sun came up. The only bright spot in this fucked up situation is I'd gotten a ton of work done already.

I'm in the kitchen waiting for Abel to wake for the day when she walks in; thank fuck she's changed out of my shirt. Although, the workout clothes she's wearing aren't much better. Tight in all the right places.

"Morning," we both say at the same time.

"There's fresh coffee in the pot, and I left a mug out for you."

"I'm going to need more than a mug to get me through today," she mutters.

"You didn't sleep either?"

"Well, let's see." She fills a mug before turning toward me. "This guy that I know keeps confusing me. One minute he's acting like I'm an irritation, the next he's holding my hand and getting me to talk about my dead parents. Then to top it off, he kisses me stupid, right before leaving me standing there alone like an idiot." My chest tightens at the confusion marring her pretty face.

"Bree ... I'm sorry. I shouldn't have done that to you." She's shocked me with how direct she is, and I'm lost for words right now.

"What are we doing here, TJ?" she asks uncertainly.

I'm saved from answering by a crying Abel. *Shit.*

I was so distracted with thoughts of Breeze that it slipped my mind that Abel was still sleeping. This is why I can't let this attraction get out of hand. I don't have room in my life for a woman. Not a woman like Breeze who could easily consume me.

"Can we talk about this later? I have to get to him."

"Of course. Go," she says softly.

"Make yourself some breakfast. I'll get him ready and we can head into work."

She doesn't answer, just smiles a smile that looks nothing like her normal smiles do. I make my way up the stairs, a conflicted mess of thoughts and feelings.

By the time I get back downstairs, she's gone, leaving behind a note that simply says:

'Something came up. See you at work. -B'

Watching the clock, I'm counting down the minutes until I get to see her again. This morning has been a bust, and it's a miracle I got anything done. My head is full of Breeze. Thoughts of kissing her. Thoughts of exploring not just her body, but what makes her tick mentally too.

Thoughts of exploring what we could be, what I want us to be.

She's due down here any minute to take Abel, and I have no idea what I'm going to say to her. I've talked myself in circles all day, and I'm no closer to knowing what it is I want.

My phone rings on the desk in front of me and for a second, I'm scared it's Breeze calling to cancel. I snatch it up, but when I see it's my brother, I decline the call. I don't have the headspace to deal with him right now.

The phone starts ringing again. There must be something wrong for Keir to call back immediately like that. Swiping the screen, I answer.

"Brother—" I don't get the chance to say anything more when he interrupts me.

"Pop's water broke. She's in labor." Instead of sounding excited, he sounds terrified. I had a feeling this would happen. He's been pretending to be okay, but secretly stressing himself out.

"What do you need from me?" I ask, jumping to my feet, ready to get to him if he needs me.

"I don't know what to do. I'm freaking out. What if she's not okay? What if—"

"I'm on my way. Stay calm. Text me the details," I tell him before hanging up the phone.

I'm almost done strapping Abel into his seat when Breeze walks into the room.

"Hey. What's going on? Where are you going?"

"Keir called. Poppy went into labor, and he needs me there. He's freaking out."

"What will you do with Abel?"

"I guess I can drop him to my mom. She'll have Chase with her anyway."

"Let me keep him," she says immediately.

"What?"

"He was supposed to be with me this afternoon anyway. Drop us off at your place then go to the hospital."

"You'd do that?"

"Of course," she says, an incredulous look on her face, like I'm stupid for not asking her before she had the chance to offer.

There are so many things I want to say to her right now. I want to go to her, wrap my arms around her, and hold on tight. Instead, I exhale the breath I always seem to be holding onto when I'm near her.

"Thank you." The soft smile she gives me is almost enough to knock me on my ass.

When I walked away from her this morning, I was glad of the distraction. Happy to have a few minutes to collect my thoughts, except all I was able to think about was the feel of her lips on mine. Seeing her again, standing right in front of me, is just making that craving stronger.

"We still need to talk," I tell her. She pauses slightly where she's made herself busy getting the rest of Abel's stuff together, but she doesn't look my way.

"It's fine," she says, trying to brush me off. "I thought about it, and you were right"—she finally looks at me before continuing—"but you were also wrong," she adds, confusing me.

"About what?"

She stares at me before answering, the conflict of whether to continue this conversation plays out right there on her face. I guess she decides to commit to it when she clears her throat and squares her shoulders before she speaks again.

"You said you shouldn't have kissed me. You're right. You shouldn't have. But you're not the only one to blame. I shouldn't have let you."

"Bree, I—"

"It's fine, TJ. It was a mistake. Let's not make it into something it doesn't need to be." Turning back to what she was doing, she effectively dismisses me.

I should be grateful. This is what I should want. She's giving me a 'get out of jail free' card. I can walk away now, before this situation can get anymore fucked up.

Except, I'm not so sure that's what I want anymore.

BREEZE

Oh shit.

"What's wrong?" Fleur asks, concern in her voice. I must have said that out loud.

"He's wearing sweatpants," I whisper into the phone that's tucked between my shoulder and my ear. I have no idea why when he's over the other side of the room and can't hear me.

"And?" Fleur prompts.

I haven't taken my eyes off TJ since I walked into the gym and saw him like this. My hungry gaze travels over every inch of him as he pulls himself up on the metal bar. Every muscle flexes and dances under his smooth skin. I'm aware that I'm staring at his ass like it's a piece of meat, but I just can't seem to drag my eyes off him.

Forcing down a whimper that's desperate to escape, I finally answer my friend, "They're gray sweatpants."

"Holy. Shit," she whispers back.

"Yep."

"Front or back view?" she asks.

"Back," I reply, silently thanking the Lord that it's just the back. I'd be likely to faint if I had to see him front on.

"Take   a   picture."
"Fleur!" I splutter a laugh. "No way, that's so inappropriate."
"I'll pay you," she offers. As much as I'm tempted to take a picture for my own needs, there's no way I'm chancing it. I'd die if I ever got   caught   with   it.
"Not happening, Fleur. But he works out this time every day, didn't you say you have to stop by tomorrow to drop that thing off?"

"I like your way of thinking." She sounds as if she's actually considering turning up here tomorrow just to ogle TJ.

Saying goodbye to my friend, I quickly make my way around the edge of the room, hoping to avoid him. It's been almost a week since Poppy had the baby, and thankfully I've managed to avoid the conversation TJ thought we needed to have.

With Keir being at home with Poppy and their new baby, TJ has been slammed here at the gym. It's been easy to keep out of his way while he's been distracted. Judging by the text he sent me early this morning, my time might be running out.

We still need to talk.

I don't need to hear him say that kissing me was a mistake. Not again. The first time hurt enough. I'd rather just forget it ever happened.

Later that evening, I'm sitting in Poppy's kitchen holding her brand new baby boy. When I started working for Keir, I didn't expect to become friends with his wife, but after coming to some of my classes, Poppy pretty much demanded my number and strong armed me into being her friend. Not that I'm complaining, she's one of the sweetest people I've ever met.

"He's adorable," I whisper, unable to take my eyes off the little boy wrapped in a white blanket she'd dropped in my arms as soon as I walked in the door. "No name yet?" I ask.

"No. We can't seem to agree." She rolls her eyes as she speaks, "Keir has terrible taste in names."

"I do not," Keir says as he walks into the kitchen where we're sitting around the table.

"Naming our son after a football player equals terrible taste in my opinion. And the poor thing will get bullied in school."

"And naming him after a 'book boyfriend' is okay?" He air-quotes the words as he speaks, making me giggle. This is obviously a conversation they've had more than once.

"There's nothing wrong with my book boyfriends! Anyway, the day you push one of your almost ten-pound babies out of your penis is the day you get the final say on its name." Poppy's pithy return makes Keir wince.

"I suppose you have a point," he mumbles, looking horrified at the thought.

"What do you think, Breeze? You grew up with an unusual name, do you like it?"

"I never really thought about it much," I tell her honestly. "My siblings and I all have unusual names, so I guess it was normal to me." Staring down at the sleeping baby, I let my mind wander to my mom and how she'd explained all our unusual names to me.

"She was a dreamer. A nomad soul that wanted to live her own version of a fairy tale. When that wasn't possible, she made her own fairy tale life with us at home. I think that's what got her through having to give up on her dreams." Hearing Poppy's soft sniffle has me looking up. She wipes away a tear before shaking her head and laughing softly.

"Ignore me and my damn baby hormones," she says as Keir wraps her up in a hug. The sound of the front door opening has us all turning to see who came in as Keir walks toward the hallway, but Chase gets there before him.

"Uncle TJ!" he yells before disappearing out of view. My eyes fly to Poppy who at least has the decency to look a little sheepish. She knows I've been avoiding him, even if she doesn't quite no why.

"Really?" I ask.

"Well, if you'd tell me why you're avoiding him, I might be more inclined to help you," she whisper-shouts at me.

I'm saved from replying when TJ walks into the room, stealing all the air as he does. Our eyes lock on each other immediately. I've been around him, but I've been able to keep our interactions limited to talk about Abel and nothing else. Now he's here, stalking toward me, and there's no Abel here to save me this time.

"Time's up, Bree," he says when he stops in front of me. Leaning down, he scoops the sleeping baby up, gives him a quick kiss on his head, and hands him off to his brother. "Let's go."

"Go?" I ask, watching as his eyes narrow on me.

Looking at him standing in front of me with those large hands of his planted on his hips, he looks like he's gearing up for a fight.

I don't know whether to climb him like a tree or kick him in the balls.

"I warned you, Breeze. Time's up. We're talking. Today."

"Oh crap. He full named her," Poppy stage whispers to Keir from somewhere behind me.

Heat creeps up my cheeks, and if I'm honest with myself, it's not from embarrassment. There's something about that commanding tone that just does it for me.

There's something wrong with me, I'm sure.

"And I told you there's nothing to talk about." I'm aiming for standoffish, but I doubt I'm fooling anyone right now, not when I can't even fool myself. Gathering my jacket and bags, I decide it's time for me to leave. "Thank you, guys, for inviting me over. The baby is adorable." I give Poppy a light hug, whispering that I'll pay her back later for this, then say goodbye to Keir and Chase.

By the time I make it to the front door, I realize that TJ is letting me walk away, and I can't deny that it stings.

I need to get a grip on myself when it comes it to that man. One minute I'm telling him that we have nothing to talk about, the next I'm wishing he wouldn't give up so easily. I'm a mess over him, and I don't like it.

Stopping at the edge of the house where I parked the bicycle I rode here; I do a double take when I see the empty space where it used to be.

"You really should lock that thing up." His deep voice sounds from right behind me, causing me to jump half out of my skin.

"TJ! Stop sneaking up on me like that!"

"Bike's in the truck. Let's go," he grunts at me.

"There's no point asking you to give it back is there?"

His hard-set features soften, and the corner of his mouth tips up in the tiniest of smirks.

"Babe," he says, as if it's a whole sentence. I let him lead me toward the big black truck that's parked across the driveway. I can do this, I lie to myself as I open the door, his hand resting on my lower back as I climb up, the heat permeating through the layers of clothing. He might as well be touching my bare skin.

"What did you want to talk about?" I ask once he's in his seat and he's started to drive.

"Later," is his only reply.

It's not until we've been on the road for a few minutes that I realize he's going the wrong way.

Wherever we're going, it's in the opposite direction of my apartment.

Nineteen

TJ

Sitting this close to her, feeling her confused stare at me through the dim evening light, is almost enough to have me pulling this damn truck over on the side of the road so I can kiss the shit out of her.

I've spent all week trying to work out what the hell I'm doing when it comes to her, and every single thought came back to the same thing.

I want her.

I have no idea what that means, what could possibly happen, but I know one thing for sure. I want her around me as much as possible.

"Where are we going?" she asks as soon as she realizes we're going the opposite direction of her place.

"Some place where you can't avoid me," I answer without looking at her, but the truth is I have no idea where I'm going. I was sitting at home, stewing over the fact that she's been avoiding me, when Poppy texted to tell me Breeze was over there. Then I was in my truck and on my way to get her.

"Where's Abel?" She shifts in her seat, tucking one leg under the other so she's facing me. It's a fight not to look at her.

"My mom has him."

"Oh," she says flatly, something like disappointment in that one word. She doesn't say anything else, but I feel her eyes on me as I finally realize where I'm headed.

"Where are we?"

Parking and shutting off the engine, I take in the sight just outside the window. I didn't plan to come here, but once I was on the road, I knew this would be the perfect place to bring her. We're only a few miles from my house, but it's like we're the only people in the whole town from up here. We're on a small bluff that looks down over the neighborhood. We're too late to see the sunset, but the clear night means the city lights are bright. The stars are gleaming above us.

Taking off my seatbelt, I open my car door and climb out of the truck. I make my way around to open the passenger door. Breeze doesn't say anything as I hold out a hand to help her down.

"Oh wow," she whispers, almost to herself. "This is beautiful."

"Stunning."

She looks at me, a glint of knowing in her eye; she must know I'm not talking about the view.

"Why did you bring me here?"

Isn't that just the million-dollar question?

Taking her perfect hand in mine, I lead her to the back of the truck, opening the tailgate and lifting her to sit up there.

"Honestly, I have no idea why I brought you here." I sigh. "I used to come up here to clear my head. I went through some stuff before Abel came along, didn't always make the best decisions," I tell her without giving away too much. I don't think she needs to hear that I was up here pining for Lucy. "Coming up here, looking down on all that"—I gesture to the tiny houses below us—"puts into perspective how small we really are."

"I can see that," she murmurs, laying back in the bed of my truck. She doesn't care she could be getting dirty. "Those stars don't even look real. They're so bright."

Moving so I'm lying next to her, I try to sort my thoughts.

"I was wrong to say that I shouldn't have kissed you." I don't take my eyes off the stars, but I feel hers on me again.

"Don't apologize—" she starts, but I have to interrupt her.

"I'm not apologizing, Bree. I'm not sorry for kissing you. I was wrong for telling you it shouldn't have happened." I sigh. "I thought pushing you away before anything could really happen was for the best."

"Why?" She props herself up on one elbow so she can look down at me.

"I told you Abel was the result of a one-night stand, but I didn't tell you that at the time it happened, I wasn't in a good place. I had no business being anywhere near Willow that night." Unable to bear the sad look on her face for another minute, I sit up and drop my head into my hands.

I can't look at her if I want to keep talking.

Pulling in a breath, I tell her something that I've been keeping locked up tight for too long now. "I was drunk and angry a lot of the time. I got mixed up in some underground fights. It wasn't a good time for me." Part of me wishes I could just stop speaking. I'd rather talk about anything other than that night, but I know that's not how this works.

"I took advantage of her. It's because of me she's dead." I brace myself, waiting for her disgust to show; instead, I feel a gentle hand on my back. Her touch doing more to sooth me than anything else has in a long time. It's a feeling I can easily see myself becoming addicted to.

"Why are you blaming yourself?" she asks, and I tell her about the night I still have a hard time remembering clearly.

"Willow was drunk. I should have known better. Should have stopped things before it got as far as it did."

"You were drunk too, right? I assume you both wanted it to happen?"

"Yeah, but—" It's Bree's turn to cut me off before I can finish.

"You can't blame yourself. What happened was tragic, but, TJ, that doesn't make it your fault." Anger blooms inside me. She doesn't get it. She doesn't fucking understand.

"You wouldn't be saying that if you knew the full story." I lean forward so her hand is no longer touching me.

"I doubt that's true," she says angrily. The only answer I can give is a derisive snort.

"So you'd still say that if you knew that Abel's mom never planned to tell me he existed?" Just saying the words cut me up, but I can't stop. "

She hated me so much that she was willing to be a single mom rather than to tell me about Abel.

Now tell me again that I did nothing wrong!"

To say she looks shocked is an understatement, but instead of being repulsed like I expected, she shifts closer to me, letting her legs dangle off the end of the tailgate next to mine. Close enough for me to feel the warmth of her body on mine. "I treated her like dirt and because of that, I wasn't there when she found out she was having him, wasn't there for any doctor appointments. I did nothing when she got sick, and she was alone when she died. All because of me. So save your sympathy for someone who deserves it."

I don't want to see the pity on her face. The last thing I need is more of that. I don't deserve it. She surprises me by staying silent for a minute before saying the very last thing I expect.

"Maybe you're right. Maybe she did think you weren't good enough." Shuffling closer, she softens her voice before continuing. "Or maybe she was scared. Maybe she didn't want to deal with a baby daddy for the next eighteen years. Maybe she was an absolute idiot." Wrapping her hand around my arm, she squeezes gently. "Or maybe, just maybe, she was scared and made a mistake. She didn't know you. Didn't know the man you are really, deep down inside."

Staring at her, I absorb her words like a sponge.

I want to believe her. I'm tired of the guilt.

I want to wake up each day without the incessant cloud that seems to be over me. Looking down to where her hand holds mine, I read the words I haven't noticed until now that are tattooed on her wrist.

Carpe Diem.

Seize the day.

I want that. I want to live in each day, not being dragged down by the past.

I can't find any words to explain how her words have affected me, how she's affected me, so I do the next best thing.

I slide my fingers along her jaw and under the hair at the nape of her neck. Cupping the back of her head, holding her where I want her, I do the one thing I've been thinking of all week. I take her lips with mine. Her eyes flare in the split second before we make contact, and I see the same need reflected at me.

God.

I want to fucking devour her. Her taste drives me wild. I can't keep this kiss soft and gentle like the first one, and our lips part as my tongue seeks hers.

This. This is what I've been craving.

The peace she brings me. I'm not letting any of the other bullshit in when she's in my arms.

By the time the kiss slows, both of my hands are on her face, and he hands grip my wrists like she doesn't want me to let go.

I feel the same way.

Twenty

BREEZE

Saying goodbye to the last people to leave my class, I switch the calming instrumental music to a more upbeat playlist. Busying myself with packing away the yoga mats, it's a struggle to keep my eyes from wandering to the clock.

It's almost time for me to head downstairs to watch Abel for a few hours. It's been three days since TJ essentially kidnapped me from Poppy's house, and we've exchanged a few text messages and a late-night phone call since, but this will be the first time seeing him in the flesh.

I can still feel the weight of his arms holding me in place, feel his lips on mine.

When he drove me home, he said goodnight with a scorching kiss, hot enough to leave me with the female equivalent of blue balls. I've been on cloud nine ever since.

I'm singing and dancing along to the music while rolling the last of the mats up when a large, warm hand wraps around my waist, and I'm pulled back into a deliciously solid body.

"You better not let my boss see you in here. I hear he doesn't like people flirting on company time." I try to joke, but it comes out more like a satisfied purr. I don't even recognize myself right now.

"Your boss is an ass." TJ's hot breath tickles my ear, causing goose bumps to race over my skin. He presses a kiss just below my ear right before he turns me in his arms.

"Hi."

"Hi." He grins back at me.

"Where's Abel?" I ask when I notice he's alone.

"Asleep downstairs, Jonah is with him. I needed five minutes alone with you."

I slide my hands up his arms and around his neck, relishing in the feel of him.

"Alone, huh?" I tease.

"Yeah, so I can do this without an audience," he says, just before his lips land on mine.

There's no slow burn this time. It's an immediate lip bruising, breath stealing kiss. He kisses me like it's all he's been able to think about for days.

By the time he slows it down, I've been backed against the closest wall, TJ's hands are gripping my ass, and I can feel a definite erection digging into my lower belly.

Holy shit.

There's something inherently sexy about him being so turned on just from a kiss.

"I haven't been able to think of anything but you ever since I walked away from your apartment," he groans, burying his face in my neck. My hands move up to his head so my fingers can sift through his hair.

"Fuck," he groans again as his arms convulse around me. "That feels amazing."

"You feel good," I reply, lost in the moment with him.

"Tell me you're free tonight." He lifts his head out of my neck so he can look at me, eyes scanning over my face.

"Why?"

"Because I need to see you, and not just for five minutes at work."

"I can be free tonight," I say, melting further into him. "What do you have planned?"

"You'll see." He smirks before he drops one last kiss on my lips. Unfortunately for me, it's not as hot as the earlier kiss, but it's still makes my toes curl.

"What are you two doing?"

Keeping a tiny baby like Abel entertained in a boring office like this isn't all that easy. He quickly grew tired of his toys, so for the last ten minutes we've been on the floor on his playmat. I've got my phone in one hand raised over my head, and I'm making Abel giggle by making stupid faces into the camera, filters on both our faces. At the sound of TJ's voice, we both swing our heads to look at him. Abel squeals when he sees his dad, little chubby legs kicking in excitement.

"This kid is a Snapchat natural," I tell TJ as he picks his son up. I don't think I could ever get tired of seeing him like this. He's already attractive, but something about him holding that baby is just ... more. He's just so much more.

"You ready to get out of here?" he asks, holding out a hand to help me up.

"Do I have time to go home and change?" I ask.

"You don't need to change." He gets Abel strapped in and ready to go.

"You're really not going to tell me where we're going?"

"Are you always this bad with surprises?" he asks, picking up both Abel's baby bag and my backpack.

"Yes. Now tell me," I say, causing him to laugh. I realize then that although I've seen him smile, he doesn't really laugh. It's a shame because his whole face lights up when he does. Happy suits him, and catching a glimpse of it makes me even more determined to do whatever it takes to make him laugh more often.

Once we're loaded into the truck, bike and all, I let myself enjoy how normal it feels, being here with them.

"I should have asked earlier, but are you okay with Abel being with us? I'd rather not leave him unless it's absolutely necessary," CJ asks without looking in my direction. Is he worried that I might say no?

"Well, seeing as he's your son, I kinda assumed he'd be with us," I tell him honestly, and he seems to relax at my answer.

"Good. Dinner at my place okay? Figured you might like a look at that lake in the daylight," he says.

"Sounds perfect."

Twenty-one

TJ

After we've finished eating, Breeze suggests we take a walk down to the water. Being here with her, it's like I'm only just seeing how beautiful the house I bought is. I was so desperate to find a decent house to bring Abel home to that I picked the first one my mom showed me. I wanted something clean and safe for him, neither of which my old apartment was. Seeing it now through Breeze's eyes, I can see how nice it is here. There are only a few other houses that have a yard that back onto the water like mine. Maybe I'll get a small boat like they all seem to have. I can already imagine a five or six-year-old Abel, wearing a life jacket, Breeze there with us. Wind blowing in all that hair of hers.

As quickly as I imagine it, the daydream fades with the realization that she might not be here then. She'll be leaving soon and so far, she's not once mentioned for how long.

"It's really beautiful out here," Breeze says as she curls up in the chair on the back deck. Abel squeal as if he's answering her and bangs a little baby fist in the edge of his jumperoo, making us both laugh at him.

"How are you not tired yet?" I ask my son, lifting him into my arms. "You like having Bree here, huh?" he answers with another squeal. "Me too, kid," I tell him, turning to see her roll her eyes at me. "You okay out here while I get him into bed?" I ask.

"I'll be fine, go." She stands, giving Abel a kiss on his head. Taking the chance while I see it, I lean in and steal a kiss from her too.

Taking Abel into the house, I somehow manage to get him bathed and into bed in record time. He's fussier than usual, but we've had a busy evening, and I'm hoping he goes to sleep quickly. Although I was sure Bree wouldn't care that he was with us tonight, it was a huge relief to hear her say the words out loud. I never thought I'd attempt to date while he's still so small, but I realized it's pointless fighting whatever this thing with Breeze is.

Once he's asleep, I grab the monitor and make my way downstairs. I didn't have time to plan anything special for tonight, but I have an idea that I really hope Bree will like.

It doesn't take long to get things organized before I head out to the deck. Breeze is still sitting in the same place. She has her feet tucked up under her, her Kindle on her lap, but her gaze is on the view in front of her. The sun is touching the horizon in the distance, just about to disappear. The evening breeze lifts her hair gently, and it hits me how badly I want to see her here like this every single day.

"Hey." Breeze turns to me, a smile on her face. My legs move in her direction before I even realize it. Standing in front of her, I hold out my hand for her to take. There's no hesitation. She lets me pulls her to her feet and into my arms. I kiss her, just because I can. It's a struggle to stop it from escalating, but I don't want her to think I brought her here just for this. Even if my dick is screaming that it wouldn't complain if that's where the night is heading.

"Come on, let's get inside before it gets cold out here." Once we're inside, I lead her toward the den. The lights are dimmed, the coffee table has been pushed to the side, and I've pulled all the cushions off the sofa. The TV is ready to play a movie, and I have a tray full of snacks laid out.

It might not be a candlelit, romantic dinner, but it's the best I can do tonight.

"TJ," Breeze gasps softly, "when did you manage to do all this?"

"Do you like it?" I ask, suddenly worried that she'll find it too juvenile.

"It's perfect." She stretches up on tiptoes, smiling brightly before pressing her lips to mine.

"Thank you."

"No problem."

Once we're settled in, I pass Bree the remote control telling her to pick whatever movie she wants. I have a feeling I'll be watching her more than whatever she picks anyway.

"You sure you trust me with this?" she sasses. "I might have to introduce you to some more classic romance."

"Whatever makes you happy, doll," I say, pulling her closer to me.

Not even ten minutes into the movie and I'm pretty sure this is the dumbest shit I've ever thought of. Instead of watching the television, I'm consumed with the perfect little body that's cuddled into my side. She's tucked under my arm, and my fingers trail up and down the bare skin of her shoulder.

Why did I ever think I could be this close to her without wanting to rip all the clothes off her perfect little body? Running my fingers down her bare arm once more, I take a small detour instead of tracing my way back up. This time I run my fingers up her side, along her waist, and across the side of her tit. She inhales a breath, and her body arches into my touch. Feeling bold I do it again. She tips her head back and looks at me with so much want on her face. I'm sure she sees the same look on my own face. Her mouth opens slightly, and I take it as the invitation I hope it is dropping down to kiss her. Her hands wrap around the back of my head, and she kisses me with a heat like I've never felt.

Fuck.

This is a battle for dominance. Her tongue flicks out to meet mine, and she uses her grip on me to pull herself up. All without once breaking our connection.

She shifts, her legs settling over my thighs as she straddles me, and the heat from her body causes my already eager cock to harden to the point of pain. My hands slide down her waist to cup her peachy ass. The ass I knew would fit perfectly in my palms. I can't help but grind my hips into hers.

Jesus.

She feels fucking phenomenal.

Dragging my lips away from hers, I can't help but feel smug as shit at the unhappy groan she lets out at the loss of contact. I don't give her a chance to complain; instead, I drag my lips down over her jaw, neck, and collarbone. Fuck me, she tastes incredible. My mouth is just about to hit the swell of her glorious tits when she shifts away from me a few inches. I get a look at her, and what I see causes my chest to tighten. Her kiss-drunk expression, swollen lips, and heaving chest make her the sexiest thing I've ever seen. I need her naked and under me right now.

"You're fucking perfect," I groan into her mouth. She doesn't answer, just drops her hands to the hem of her shirt before she rips it over her head. She's got her hands under my shirt before hers even hits the floor.

Thank fuck she's as hungry for this as I am.

I'm yanking the button on her jeans open when I hear the only thing that could tear me away from Breeze right now.

Abel.

His soft cries filter from the monitor that's on the side table next to us. Breeze freezes in my arms before she reaches over and turns the small screen toward us. Yeah, my boy is wide awake.

Letting my head drop back on the pillows, I stifle the urge to curse.

"I'm sorry," I tell her. "He doesn't usually wake up like this." Before I can move away, she grabs my face in her hands.

"Don't apologize. You have a tiny baby, they wake up. It's fine, we can finish this another time." She smiles at me softly, and it hits me somewhere deep that she really means it. She's not fazed by the interruption at all.

"Let me go settle him. Will you stay?"

"If you're sure?" she asks.

"Babe, never been more sure," I tell her, dropping a kiss on her mouth before I make my way upstairs to my son.

Twenty-Two

BREEZE

"This isn't exactly what I had planned for tonight, you know," TJ whispers close to my ear, startling me.

Glancing down at the baby sleeping on my chest, I can't help but smile.

"It's been perfect," I say, and I don't know if I've ever been more honest.

When Abel woke up fussing earlier, I made the mistake of going to his bedroom with TJ. The minute he saw me, his little chubby arms reached for me. There was no way he was going to fall asleep with me there. Instead, I suggested we bring him downstairs with us to finish the movie. Sure, I might not be getting the happy ending I was expecting, but I wasn't lying when I said it's been a perfect night. All of it.

Laying here tucked in close to TJ, Abel asleep between us, I feel something I didn't realize I've been missing from my life.

Contentment.

It's a peaceful feeling that I know I could easily get addicted to.

"Do you want me to carry him up?" TJ asks.

"I've got him," I reply, trying not to jostle the baby as I stand. I carry him upstairs and gently place him in his crib. Grabbing his blanket, I make sure he's tucked in. He really is the most beautiful little boy. I see so much of TJ in him, and I can already tell he's going to be leaving broken hearts left, right, and center when he's older.

"Night, gorgeous boy," I whisper before turning to leave the room. I'm not surprised when I see TJ leaning against the doorframe, watching me. He takes my hand in his and leads me downstairs where I notice he's picked up the cushions and the room is back to normal. Does this mean he wants me to leave? I don't get a chance to ask him before he pulls me down onto the sofa, where he once again settles me as close to his side as possible. Picking up the remote, he presses play on the last part of the movie.

I can't deny that part of me is disappointed. We'd been going at each other with an intensity unlike anything I've ever experienced right before Abel interrupted us. I might not be a virgin, but I've never felt that kind of heat with another person before. I was kind of hoping we'd pick up where we left off. Now I have no idea where his head is at. Does he not want me as much as I want him?

"What are you thinking so hard about?" he asks.

"Nothing." I opt not to tell him that I'm disappointed he isn't stripping me out of my clothes right this second.

"Why are you so tense then?"

"I'm not tense," I lie, not taking my eyes off the screen. Instead of pushing me to answer, TJ shifts me so my back is flat on the sofa. Hovering over me, he stares right into my eyes. He slowly drops his mouth to mine, soft lips kissing first my top lip, then the bottom one.

It's mesmerizing, being this close to him, feeling the weight of him on me.

As always with us, the kiss quickly ignites.

Hands start to roam, tongues trace skin, hips start to grind.

My hands are on the button of his jeans, determined to finally get them off this time. Once I have the button yanked open, I slide my hands inside and grip his cock in both hands. Ripping his mouth away from mine, he buries his head into my neck and growls, *"Fuck."*

The vibration of his voice, coupled with the feel of his breath dancing over my heated skin, causes my entire body to clench. Sparks fly behind my closed eyes. It's thrilling, knowing that I can get this usually cool, calm, and collected man to react this way. I want him to feel what I'm feeling. This heady mix of powerful and powerless. When I open my eyes, the look I see staring back at me tells me he's maybe already feeling it.

"You sure about this, baby?" Lifting himself off me slightly, his eyes bore into mine. The heat I see in there is enough. I'm beyond sure. I might have no idea what this thing is between us or where it's going to take us, but I do know that I want him. Need him. More than I need my next breath, I need to feel him inside of me.

"Please," I beg, but the words are cut off when TJ yanks my pants off me, my shirt and bra following quickly behind.

This time it's my turn to groan. It's like he can't decide which part of me he wants to devour first. His mouth finds my nipple, and he sucks on it, hard. My nails rake the skin on his muscled back, and my legs hook around his thighs, trying my damnedest to get him to move closer to me.

"Patience," he says, letting my breast go with a pop. His lips quickly land in the center of my chest where he drops open-mouth kisses, slowly making his way down to my stomach. I think I might combust before he even reaches his intended destination.

He doesn't slow down when he reaches the apex of my thighs; he pushes them wider apart and dives in and gives me one long lick before latching onto my clit and sucking hard.

"Holy shit!" I exclaim. My head drops back, and my eyes roll back in my head. I'm not going to last much longer, an orgasm already beginning to dance through me. The second he brings one of his talented, thick fingers into play, I see stars.

My body tightens, toes curl, and the fingers of one hand fight for purchase on the sofa beneath me, while the others tug on his hair. Then comes the bliss. The waves and waves of pleasure that carry me away. I'm vaguely aware of TJ kissing his way up my body, each press of his lips sending yet more shocks through me.

"That was fucking beautiful." I pry my eyes open at his words. He leans over me, strong corded arms caging me in, swollen lips and hair a mess.

As sated as I should feel after that, I'm still burning for him, burning to feel him.

"I need you."

"You have me, baby," he says as he takes his heavy cock in hand and rubs it through my folds. Shifting back so he's on his knees between my legs, he continues to tease me. I'm too mesmerized by the sight of him to complain at the loss of contact.

"I need to see this," he tells me, never taking his eyes off where he's still teasing me. I'm about to lose my mind.

"TJ ... please," I beg, bucking my hips, hoping he'll hurry up and fill me. He takes one hand and presses down on my thigh, pushing my legs open wider.

And then he's sliding inside me. Just the tip to start. A few inches in. A few inches out. Over and over again. It's the sweetest torture as he rocks his hips in tiny movements.

"Let me see you play with your tits, Breeze." Reaching up, I play with my nipples, needing something to help ease the ache he's created deep within me.

"Fuck ... you're so fucking beautiful like that; pull them harder," he groans before he slides all the way in. His head drops back on his shoulders, and he stays planted inside me for what feels like minutes. I can't help it when I clench down on him; the sight of him so affected by me is the biggest turn on. When he finally moves, it's slow, deliberate pumps.

He wraps his arms around my waist and lifts me so we're chest to chest, faces barely a breath apart, my legs wrapped tightly around him. The new position means he can hit somewhere deep inside where I don't think anyone else has ever touched. All the while he keeps his eyes boring into mine. It's like he's trying to communicate without words.

"I could fucking live inside you," he says against my lips before his tongue slides into my willing mouth. The tempo of his thrusts increases, like he's unable to control it any longer. He pumps harder, faster. Over and over, hitting that sweet spot deep inside me.

"Best. Fucking. Ever," he grits out between thrusts. "So close, Bree ... baby ... fuck, you need to come soon."

Burying my head in his neck, I let go for the second time. This climax is no less shattering than the first. But this time I get to see TJ fall over the edge with me. Tipping my head back, I drink in the sight of his dark eyes turning liquid, the tendons in his neck standing out as his body tenses. I feel his release as it thunders from him, into me.

His eyes never drop from mine. Not even when he repositions us so he's flat on his back and I'm draped over him. Not when he cups my face and drops a precious kiss on my lips.

"You ok?" he asks, and all I can do is smile. I can't answer with words, too consumed with the feelings he's evoked in me.

Words are beyond me; I've been reduced to whimpers and sighs.

Euphoria. I'm pretty sure that's what this is.

I've never felt it before and right now, all I can think of is feeling it again as soon as possible.

Twenty-three

TJ

"Why are you standing here?" Keir asks, stopping next to me outside of the studio where Breeze is currently playing on the floor with Abel. I've been watching them for a while, and the sight is addicting.

"Creeping on the staff, bro? Really?" he says, punching me in my arm.

"I'm not creeping. And she's not just staff," I tell him without turning away from the view in front of me.

"She's not, huh?" His reply sounds smug. He knows there's something going on. We might not have talked about it, but he's my twin. He knows me better than anyone.

"Why are you even here?" I finally turn to face him. He's supposed to be at home with Poppy and the boys for another week at least.

"I told Lucy I'd get some stuff done for her. Have you noticed anything off with her? She didn't sound like herself when she called last night."

"I haven't seen much of her," I tell him. We might be on decent terms now, but Lucy and I were toxic together for a long time. I don't know if we'll ever be able to get to a place where she can call me if she has something going on.

"Can you keep an eye on her for me? Poppy is worried about her too."

"Sure, will do." My attention shifts back to watching Breeze through the window. She's down on her knees on the floor, Abel on the yoga mat in front of her. She's holding his little hands and moving his arms to the beat of the music. His legs are kicking everywhere, and I can hear his chuckles over the music.

That sound. It fills parts of me that I didn't realize were cracked. He might have come into my life in the most unexpected way, but there hasn't been a day of his life that I haven't loved that little boy.

"What are they doing?" Keir asks, reminding me that he's still there.

"Yoga." I deadpan.

"Obviously." I can practically hear the eyeroll in his tone. "You can do that with a baby? We should look into setting up something like this for members. She's good." I don't answer. He must have forgotten that Breeze won't be here long enough to set up anything like that.

We watch as she does some sort of press up over my son, dropping down far enough to kiss his head each time. My eyes rove over her curves that are encased in tight workout gear. Inappropriate while she's looking after my son? Probably. But with a body like hers it's inevitable. She stretches one toned leg out, alternating left to right each time she leans down. Maybe I can get her to try this later, but with me underneath her instead.

She leans over, laughing along with my boy before she drops one final kiss on his head, like it's the most natural thing in the world. Leaning forward to scoop him up, Bree moves so she's sitting crossed legged in front of the floor to ceiling mirrored wall. She places Abel in the crook of her lap and wraps her arms around his belly. Closing her eyes, she takes some deep breaths. This isn't the first time I've watched this. The two of them do yoga together happens every time she watches him, and he seems to get as much out of it as she does. Less than a minute into her meditation and Abel is almost asleep, her deep, even breathing soothing him.

Seeing Breeze make him so happy makes me imagine a future I'm not sure I have any business imagining. Whatever it is we're doing doesn't have a label. I was attracted to her from the first time I set eyes on her outside my office, but after getting her into my bed and underneath me last week, she has consumed me. We've spent every night together, and I've made it my mission to find out what makes her tick. And not just in the bedroom. I know we need to talk. I should be asking her what she has planned, but deep down I'm scared of her answer. What if she's leaving and never coming back? She's only been in my life for a few weeks, and already I know that she'll leave behind a hole that I'm not sure I'll ever be able to fill.

"Am I making a mistake?" I ask Keir.

"With what?"

"Letting her in. Letting her get close to us."

"Does it feel like a mistake?"

"No. Never," I tell him without having to think about it. "She fits. With both of us. She just fits."

"Why are you doubting it then?"

"She wants the world," I tell him, letting him know my biggest fear—that Abel and I will not be enough. That this beautiful, free spirit will feel like I clipped her wings if I tie her to us.

"Find a way to give it to her then," he says, like doing it should be the simplest thing in the world.

Then he walks away, leaving me to figure out how the fuck I'm supposed to give her the world, without breaking my heart and hers in the process.

Twenty-four

BREEZE

"Morning, baby."

The gruff voice at my ear causes my body to react on its own accord, arching into TJ's hard body as it cocoons me. The heat of his lips meets the skin of my neck and I resist the urge to purr in satisfaction.

"Morning." My reply is a breathy moan, and I hardly recognize the sound of my voice. Shifting slightly, TJ rolls me to my back. I hardly have time to appreciate how gorgeous he looks rumpled from sleep, before he swoops down to kiss me.

I could easily get used to waking up like this.

I *have* gotten used to waking up like this.

I've spent pretty much every night since our first time together here with TJ and Abel. So far, I've managed to avoid thinking too much about what we're doing here. It's especially easy to avoid those thoughts when TJ does things like what he's doing right now. Concentrating on the kisses he's dotting along my jaw and neck allows my mind to blank out everything except for him. It's only been a few hours since he was inside me last, but even that is entirely too long.

Pushing my hands against his huge shoulders, I break the connection between us and roll him to his back.

TJ spoils me. Most of our time in this bed is spent with him worshipping me. I don't get to reciprocate often enough, but this morning, I'm starving for him.

Quickly straddling him, I kiss my way down his body, hopefully making my intentions clear. I kiss over the tattoos on his chest and over his outrageous abs. When I get to the ridges that line his hips, I let my tongue peek out to trace them.

"Fuck sake, Breeze," he growls, hands sliding into my hair. Taking ahold of his solid cock, squeezing gently at first and giving him a few stokes, I revel in the way he stares at me. The heat in his eyes lets me know just how much he's struggling with letting me control the pace like this.

I'd better make the most of this because I have a feeling he's about to snap. Lowering my head, I wrap my lips around the broad head of his cock, making sure to suck gently at first. TJ rewards me with a deep, guttural moan that vibrates through his whole body. The sound turns me on even more than I already am. Taking him in deeper, I use both hands to jack the part of him that I can't fit in my mouth. He's larger than any man I've ever been with, and I can't take all of him. I don't think he cares much based on the reaction I get when he touches the back of my throat.

"That's it ... so fucking good, baby," he praises, and it spurs me on. Trying my hardest to relax my throat, I try to take him in further. Holding my head in place, he gently rocks his hips into me.

"This okay?" he asks, sounding breathless. The best I can do is moan and increase the suction.

"Shit, Bree, baby ... I'm not going to last. You need to stop if you don't want me to come in your mouth." I don't let him go when he tries to move me off him. It only takes a few more seconds for him to explode in my mouth, and the pulse of him coming against my tongue is hypnotic. I already know I can't wait to do this to him again.

Letting go of his still hard cock, he falls back against the pillow, chest heaving.

I did that to him.

Dropping my chin to his thigh, I revel in the sight of him so undone. He doesn't give me long to do so, though, as he drags me up his body.

"Thank you, baby. That was fucking incredible," he murmurs against my lips, causing my cheeks to heat. I'm saved from replying when a small shout sounds from the baby monitor next to the bed. We both turn toward the small screen where Abel can be seen in his crib, babbling to himself and trying to grab his feet.

"Looks like you'll have to wait for your turn, sorry." Giving my ass a light squeeze, TJ kisses me quickly before he gets out of the bed. "Go back to sleep. You don't have to get up for another hour yet."

Grabbing his pillow, I snuggle down into the bed and enjoy the view. I don't think I could ever get sick of watching a naked TJ walking around. Instead of going back to sleep, I decide to go and get Abel. He's not fussing, but I can't resist a morning cuddle before the craziness of the day kicks in. Pulling on one of TJ's shirts, I make my way into the nursery. Abel squeals when he sees me, arms and legs flailing.

"Morning, gorgeous boy." I scoop him up and kiss his head. Changing his diaper, I carry him to the bedroom and climb into the bed, settling him on the pillows next to me. The bathroom door opens and TJ steps out, a towel around his waist and water dripping down his chest.

"I told you to go back to sleep," He scolds, coming to sit next to me on the bed, leaning over to kiss Abel. When he does the same to me, Abel whacks him in the jaw with a sticky fist.

"Thanks, bud." He chuckles, the sound making me smile too.

"I'm not tired." I shrug.

"You have him all day today; you should make the most of your free time."

"I'd rather spend my morning with you guys."

He stares at me a beat, looking like there are words that want to fall off the tip of his tongue, but he must decide against it. Instead, he moves to the closet to get dressed, stepping out a few moments later wearing a crisp white tee and gray sweats. As much as I appreciate the view, I can't help but be jealous. I'm going to be here all day while he's at the gym looking like a snack for all the gym bunnies who want him. It's hard enough when I'm forced to see it with my own eyes, but knowing I won't be there leaves me feeling uncomfortably jealous.

"Don't you have any black sweats?" I blurt out, and I immediately want to pull my tongue out. I'm so freaking embarrassed.

"What?" he asks, looking completely bemused.

"Nothing. Ignore me," I deflect.

"You have something against gray sweats?" Judging by the light in his eyes, he's teasing me. This is new.

"I have something against other women seeing you in them," I tell him, deciding to be honest, even if it does make me sound ridiculous.

"Really?" he laughs, sounding slightly incredulous.

"You have to know that gray sweats on a hot guy can make a woman lose her mind," I reason.

"Do they do that to you?" he asks, moving to nuzzle into my neck.

"Uh-huh."

Pulling back to look into my eyes, TJ waits until he has my full attention before he speaks again. "It's just you. You know that, right? I don't see anyone but you." His voice is gentle, but there's a grit there that tells me he really wants me to trust the words.

"I know," I tell him softly.

"Good. Now let's get this guy some food before he pitches a fit." Reaching over me, he lifts Abel up and turns to go, leaving me sprawled in his bed, a big puddle of feelings.

"We drew straws while you were in the bathroom, I got the short straw. What's the deal with you and TJ?" Elliott asks just as I take a sip of my hot drink. It threatens to come flying back out as I choke. Poppy reaches over and pats me on the back. Looking around the small table we're sat at, I see Elliott and Fleur are staring at me, waiting for me to reply.

Today is the first day that TJ has left Abel with me for the full day. Not wanting to spend all day at home with him, I arranged to meet Poppy and Elliott for lunch. I suggested Deja Brew so that I could see Fleur too. We've both been so busy with work that we've not had time to catch up. Between us all, there are four babies and three strollers. Instead of taking over the small café, we've spread out over two tables in the small courtyard out back. Luckily the three small babies are sleeping, and Chase is sitting in a high chair making a mess of himself and the floor with a blueberry muffin.

"What do you mean?" I ask, hoping to deflect.

"Don't play dumb. We all saw the way he was looking at you at Pop's baby shower," Elliott says.

"Nothing is happening." I have no idea how else to answer. We've yet to have any kind of conversation about what we are or aren't. How the hell am I supposed to explain it to anyone else.

"Didn't look like nothing when he kidnapped you from my house," Poppy interrupts. Looking at the eager faces staring back at me, I relent.

"Okay." I sigh. "We're together? I think?" I don't know why it comes out as a question.

"You think?" my best friend asks.

"He's never put a label on it, but we're spending time together. A lot of time." I feel the heat hit my cheeks when I think of exactly *how* we spend most of that time together.

"Is 'spending time together' code for you getting it on the regular?" Elliott asks, but I don't get to answer when a voice speaks from behind me.

"Who's getting it on the regular?" Turning in my seat, I'm surprised to see Lucy standing there.

"You made it!" Poppy squeaks and stands to hug her friend. I don't miss the look she throws at Elliott, though, or the way Elliott bugs her eyes out in return. That's weird. Instead of dwelling on it, I shift my chair around so that Lucy can pull one up.

"What did I miss? Who's getting it regularly?" I don't know why the thought of carrying on the conversation now makes me so uncomfortable. TJ might have started to open up to me, but he hasn't really mentioned anything about whatever went on with him and Lucy. I know it was something, that was easy to see from a few pictures of them together. If they weren't in a relationship, they definitely slept together.

Bile works its way into my throat at the thought of it.

Lucy is beautiful, and she obviously has a lot in common with TJ. She's closer to him in age too. I'm not an insecure person by nature, but something about imagining them together twists my insides.

"Nobody. How have you been? I feel like I never see you anymore!" Poppy pulls the conversation back to safer topics. The fact that she sees the need to do that is telling. Why do I get the feeling she's trying to protect her friend's feelings?

The next hour passes in a blur as the other women chatter. I'm too wrapped up in my mind to pay much attention to what's going on around me. I get the feeling that Lucy wants to talk, but not while I'm here. I zone out, instead distracting myself with feeding Abel when he wakes up. Fleur goes back to work, and I feel out of place now. Like I'm an intruder.

I have no idea how a day that started out so wonderfully is ending with me feeling so out of sorts.

Twenty-five

TJ

"That boy is on fire," Hayden speaks from beside me. We're both leaning on the ropes watching Jonah work his way through his third sparring partner for the night. He's running rings around guys who have been fighting longer than he's been alive, and not just physically. He's anticipating their moves before they even make them. He's got a fire in him that is going to take him to the top.

"What brings you here this time of night?" I ask, noticing it's almost eight o'clock and he's not dressed for a workout.

"Waiting for Lucy to finish. We're going to Maggie's."

"Her man okay with you taking her on a date?" I ask, keeping my eye on the ring. I'm giving up time with Abel and Breeze to be here for Jonah, not to gossip with Hayden.

"First of all, it's not like that, and if you'd have pulled your head out of your ass last year, you would have known it was never like that between us. She's my friend. That's it," he says, sounding exasperated. "Secondly, she's going through some shit. She won't tell me what, so I plan to get her tipsy so she'll spill."

This gets my attention. I haven't noticed anything wrong with her, but it's not like we spend any real time together anymore.

"She okay? You're the second person to say that now."

"I hope so, man," he says just as his phone chirps in his pocket. "She's waiting upstairs; poker night soon?" He slaps me on the back as he leaves. Pulling my phone out, I make a note in my schedule to try to catch up with Lucy tomorrow. I'm probably the last person she wants to talk to, but it's worth a shot. If my brother and one of her best friends is concerned, there must be something up with her.

Focusing on what's happening in the ring, I try to push out all other thoughts, but my mind constantly wanders back to Bree. I've spoken to her throughout the day, but it's not the same as having her here. I missed being able to sneak upstairs to kiss her whenever I felt like it. I missed knowing she was close by.

Fuck, I just missed her.

Letting myself into the house an hour later, I'm surprised to find it's still dark in here. I texted Bree to let her know I'd be home, so I know she's here somewhere. Dumping my bag and keys, I make my way upstairs where I find her wrapped up in a blanket in the rocking chair in Abel's room. She's just sitting in the dim light, watching him sleep.

"Hey, sweetheart," I say, leaning over to kiss her.

"Hi." I can tell immediately that something is off with her. She's flat, her usual spark missing.

"What's wrong?" I ask.

"Nothing," she lies, avoiding eye contact.

"Babe,"—grabbing her chin gently, I make her look me in the eye—"speak to me."

When our eyes connect, I can feel some of the tension leave her body. I don't like seeing her wound tight like this. Dropping another quick kiss on her lips, I pull her to her feet.

"Let's go to bed."

"It's only just past nine o'clock," she says as I drag her along the hall.

"I don't care. It's been a long ass day, and I haven't kissed you properly since this morning."

Once the door is closed behind us, I yank her in to my arms and kiss the argument right out of her. She melts into me, into the kiss, and before long we're on my bed dry humping like a pair of teenagers. It kills me to do it, but I need to slow this down. Something is going on in her head, and I want to know what it is. Rolling my body on top of hers, I pin her to the bed.

"Talk to me." She tries to pull me down instead of answering me.

"I'm fine. Don't stop," she begs, hands snaking up the back of my shirt. Moving to grab her hands, I pin them to the bed next to her head. I use my hips to keep her lower half right where it is.

"Babe," I try again, "talk to me." She stares up, eyes locked on mine. The need for her to open up to me catches me off guard. "Is it Abel? Was he hard work today? If he's too much we can work—"

"It's nothing to do with Abel." She sighs but remains quiet for a minute. When she finally continues, I'm floored by her words.

"At lunch today, everyone was asking me questions about you. About us. I wasn't sure how to answer."

"How did you want to answer?"

"What do you mean?"

"I mean what I said, baby. How did you want to answer? How do you want to define what we are?"

"I don't know," she says so softly I can hardly hear her. "How would you answer?"

Well fuck if that's not a loaded question. I want to tell her that my answer would be that she's mine, always will be, end of discussion. Instead, I try to answer without scaring her off.

"I'd tell them that we're together. We're new, but we're working on building something. Something special." More of that tension drains from her features, and a small smile plays at her lips.

"Yeah?" she asks.

"Yeah," I answer with a kiss. "Was it really that hard to tell me that?"

"Well ... actually, that wasn't exactly why I was acting a little funny," she says, eyes trained on my throat instead of my face, fingers twisting in the neck of my shirt.

"Tell me," I prompt her with a squeeze, rolling us so we're face to face, propped up on pillows. "I can't fix whatever is wrong if you don't tell me what it is, sweetheart."

"Will you tell me about Lucy? You and her?" The unexpected words sound pained as they leave her lips. Like she has to ask, but she doesn't really want to hear the answer.

I can't say I'm surprised she's asking; I've been expecting it. People love to gossip, so it's a miracle she hasn't asked before now.

"I know it's none of my business, but she walked into Deja Brew right in the middle of a conversation about us, and Poppy couldn't have changed the subject any quicker. It was super awkward."

Dropping onto my back, I scrub a hand over my face. I'm not sure how to tell her about this shit.

"Lucy and I were friends for a long time." I don't look at her. It's easier this way. "We were starting up Flex, and she was around a lot. The more time we spent together, the more I became attracted to her." Bree stiffens at my honesty, but I pull her tighter to my side. I need to get this shit out so we can move on. I don't want her to doubt my feelings for her, and she's obviously worked this Lucy thing into something bigger than it is in her mind. "I thought we could be something. I thought I was ready to settle down." I stall, looking for the right way to continue.

"But..." She coaxes me to carry on.

"But I freaked out. We slept together, and instead of starting a relationship, I pushed her away. I wasn't as ready as I thought. I brushed her off and wasn't all that nice about it."

Moving closer to my side, Bree rests her chin on top of her hands on my chest.

"What happened after that?"

"She hated me," I huff out on a laugh. "She did things to get my attention; I did the same to her. Despite that, for a long time, I thought if we could get on the same page, she might be the one. You know, I thought she and Hayden had something going on? I thought she was doing it to get back at me."

"What changed?"

"She met Scott. I could see from the way that they looked at each other that it was the real deal. Whatever bullshit we had didn't matter to her anymore."

"She broke your heart." It's a statement. Not a question.

"No," I answer immediately. "I didn't realize it at first, but she never really had it to break." I pull her face closer for a kiss. Now that we're here in this moment, I decide to tell her the one thing nobody else knows. If we're going to make this work, I won't be able to keep it from her forever anyway.

"You remember I told you I was going through some shit the night I met Abel's mom?" Bree nods, but doesn't speak. "Back then, I was pissed at Lucy, pissed at the world. Pissed at myself, most of all. I thought I pushed her into the arms of someone else. I was drinking too much, partying every night, fighting more nights than I wasn't. I was trying to block all the crap out. I was set to self-destruct. Then that night, I sat in a bar and watched a woman walk in who could have been Lucy's twin sister."

"Willow," she whispers, sad eyes trained on me, waiting for me to continue.

"Willow," I confirm.

"Oh, honey."

My mind flashes back to that night. To the words that kept me awake for months after.

"It's okay. You don't have to love me. I can be her if you need me to be."

I'd called her by Lucy's name. I'd said another woman's name, and instead of pushing me away, she told me it was okay. She was so desperately looking for her own escape, she let me pretend she was someone else. And that was exactly what I did. I used her.

"TJ—" Sympathy lines her face, and I can't bear to see it. I don't deserve it. Standing from the bed, I go to my closet and pull down the small box that Willow's friend Jessie left for Abel. Digging to the bottom, I slide out the picture of Willow. It knocked me on my ass the first time I saw it. In the months after our night together, I wondered if I'd imagined the similarities between her and Lucy. Seeing this picture, I definitely wasn't wrong.

"That was a wake-up call for me. I was disgusted with myself for months afterward. Then Abel came along, and you know what happened after that," I say as I sit and hand her the picture.

"Oh wow," she says as she looks at it. "She was beautiful." Putting the picture on the bedside table, she moves to straddle my lap. Sliding her hands into my hair, she holds my face in place before she speaks. "You still blame yourself?"

"I'm trying not to, but it's not that simple, baby." I want to move on, leave the past where it is, but it's just not that easy.

"That's okay. We'll work on fixing that. Together."

Together.

Despite the look of trepidation she's doing her best to mask, I truly believe her when she says it, and I can't deny how fucking good that sounds.

Twenty-Six

BREEZE

The sound of little baby giggles fills the air of TJ's backyard. He's sitting on a blanket in the grass, and Abel is sitting in front of him, wobbling precariously. He's growing up so fast, and it feels like he's learning something new every day. He starts to lean to one side and TJ catches him, causing another wave of giggles to leave his tiny body. They're too far away for me to hear what it is TJ says to him, but Abel stares at his dad with rapt attention.

No matter what TJ thinks, he's an amazing father. I could watch these two together forever.

It hits me that I want that. I want to be here. I want to watch Abel grow. I've only been in his life for a few months, but it's impossible not to love him.

My cell phone vibrates on the table next to me. Putting down the book I was pretending to read, I see 'Asa Calling' light up my screen.

"Hey, big brother," I answer.

"So you do remember me?" he says, causing me to roll my eyes.

"Stop being dramatic. That's Ava's role in the family."

"We haven't seen you in weeks." He ignores my joke.

"I'm working a lot, Asa."

"Yeah, and you'll be gone for who knows how long soon. Your family wants to see you. Make it happen, Breeze. Soon, before Ava sends out a search party for you." It's on the tip of my tongue to tell him I'm not going. That traveling around Europe doesn't hold the same appeal that it used to. That my dreams have changed, and now they feature two dark haired guys who fill my days with happiness that I've never had before. The last few months with them have changed my view on a lot of things.

But I don't say any of that.

"I'll work something out. Later this week maybe."

"Bring the boyfriend if you have to," he says, sounding like it pains him to even make the offer.

"Maybe."

"I gotta get back to work. Love you, sis," he says before he hangs up, leaving me with a head full of thoughts I have no idea how to process.

Was it really only a few weeks ago that my mind was filled with thoughts of escaping Savannah? How easy would it be to stay? To continue whatever it is TJ and I are doing. What are we doing? He says we're building something. Something special. But that's not a label, and despite saying I don't need a label, deep down I really do.

Can I really give up a dream I've had for as long as I can remember, for a man? A man I've known for a few months?

My heart says yes. It's telling me to stay.

My brain says to be rational. He's never asked me to stay. Not once mentioned anything beyond what we have planned for the following days. Pain hits my chest at the realization that he's probably only with me *because* there's an expiration date on us. He said he wasn't ready to have a relationship while Abel was so small and needed him so much. He made an exception for me because I'm leaving. A wave of sadness washes over me, causing my stomach to lurch and my breath to catch.

The thought of me not meaning to him what he does to me kills me.

I'm pretty sure I'm in love with him. And as much as I want this, I need to be sure he wants it too.

———

"You almost ready?" TJ says against the skin of my neck. Rinsing the last of the breakfast dishes, I quickly dry my hands before turning to face him. He doesn't step back to give me room, so we end up face to face. Sliding my hands up his shoulders, I lean up to press my lips against his. He tightens his grip on me and drags my body tighter against his. It doesn't take long before I feel him harden through his jeans.

"Do we have to go?" he groans against my mouth. "We could just stay here and do more of this." He presses his hips into me.

"As amazing as that sounds, your family is waiting for us," I answer. It's Chase's birthday, and Poppy is throwing a party at their house to celebrate.

"Fine," he sulks, "but we're not staying long."

"You get Abel, I'll get the gift bag." Giving him one last kiss, I push him back a step so I can get everything ready to go.

"Gift bag?" TJ asks.

"Yeah, I picked him up a few things from us." A look passes over his face that I can't decipher.

"You got him gifts? From us?" *Crap.* I went shopping without even thinking it would be an issue. I assumed he'd be okay with it.

"They can be from me if you already got him something." I don't finish the words because I'm swept up in a tight embrace.

"Thank you, sweetheart," he says into my hair. "Means the world."

Means the world.

The words ricochet through me, leaving a trail of warmth in their wake.

"No problem," I murmur.

"I already put cash in a card for him, signed it from the both of us. That okay with you?"

"Perfect."

"Yeah, sweetheart. Perfect," he whispers against the top of my head.

"Let's get going. Abel will be ready for his nap soon, and neither of us wants to deal with a cranky baby all afternoon."

———

"Breeze, it's lovely to see you again," TJ's mom says as she sits in the chair next to me, kissing me on the cheek.

"You too, Mrs. Harmon. You guys have done an amazing job out here." The garden has been turned into little kid heaven. There are two teenage girls painting the little ones faces, a clown who's making balloon animals and swords. There's also two huge bounce houses set up. One of which currently has Hayden jumping around in it like an idiot. He looks ridiculous. There are groups of people all over the place, while more little kids than I've ever seen run wild all over the place. TJ managed to find us a couple of chairs away from the crowd, and we've spent the last hour people watching and relaxing while his mom took Abel to meet some of her friends who are inside the house.

"Thank you, but please call me Diana. Mrs, Harmon makes me feel old," she laughs. "Everyone seems to be enjoying themselves, some more than others." She rolls her eyes at Hayden who's now being tackled by a group of kids that are barely taller than his knees.

"Poppy did an amazing job," she says as she looks around at all of her family and friends with so much pride on her face. She's got Abel in her arms, but he keeps twisting to try to get to me.

"Seems my grandbaby is quite taken with you." She smirks as she passes him into my arms.

"He just knows me as the one who feeds him when his daddy is working." Laughing, I try to brush her off. Abel and I have gotten close. Even if I'm not actually babysitting for him, I'm at the house with him and TJ, more often than not.

"Whatever you say, sweetie," she laughs as she walks away from us.

"She's right. He is smitten with you," TJ says, pulling my chair closer to his a few inches. Once we're close enough, he does his usual routine of kissing Abel on his head, then kissing me softly on the lips. "I don't think he's the only one either."

"Yeah?" I can't help the smile that pulls at my cheeks. This is the first time we've been around his family all at once like this, and I wasn't sure how comfortable he'd be with being affectionate in front of them. While he hasn't exactly mauled me, he has had a hand on me most of the time. It's the little bit of reassurance that I needed after my mini freak out earlier. I know I need to talk things through with TJ, and I plan to do it very soon.

Looking down at the baby, I see he's rubbing his eye with a tiny fist. He should've had a nap by now, but between the excitement of all the kids around him, and being passed around his family, he's missed it. I know him well enough to know that an over tired Abel isn't a pretty sight. This boy needs a nap.

"I'm going to put him down for an hour," I tell TJ before standing and hitching Abel up higher on my hip, grabbing his bag to hang on the other shoulder.

"You want me to take him?" he offers, but I tell him I've got it. I have managed to perfect the art of getting this boy to sleep in record time.

As we walk, Abel buries his face into my chest and wraps one of his hands up in my hair. "Let's get you to sleep, sweet boy," I coo, kissing his head as I make my way to the small room Poppy has set up for the babies to nap in. It's only a few yards away from where we're sitting, and I can see the door from my seat. The Pack-n-Play is set up, so I just have to lay him down and wait for him to go to sleep. Pulling the blinds closed to darken the room slightly, I make sure his blanket is tucked in tight, just how he likes it. I'm about to close the door when I realize, I haven't set up the monitor I've brought from TJ's house. Plugging it in, I'm surprised when sounds from outside blare from the small unit in my hand. I must have picked up the wrong unit. I'm about to turn down the volume so it doesn't disturb the baby when voices filter through. Curiosity wins, and I lift the speaker to my ear so I can hear what's being said. I recognize TJ's deep, rumbling voice immediately, but the other one is too quiet.

Moving to the window, I shift the blind so I can see who it is he's speaking to. The beautiful brunette standing next to TJ shifts to the side so I can see her face. I don't need to see her. I already knew it was Lucy.

My stomach pitches as she sits in my seat. The seat that's still pulled close to him. I can't take my eyes off them. It's unsettling how good they look sitting next to each other, how well they seem to fit. I'm back to feeling like an intruder as I watch them. They're sitting there in silence, but I can't drag my eyes away.

"Do you ever think about us?"

The volume is low on the monitor, but the words are still like a whip cracking in the silent room.

My heart seizes at the question. My worst fears are playing out right in front of me.

He doesn't answer right away, keeping his eyes trained on the party that's still in full swing in front of him.

"Yeah, Luce. I do," he laughs, but even distorted through the tiny speaker, I can tell there's no humor in it.

"You fucked me up," he tells her, and tears well in my eyes at his words. Words I've already heard from him but feel all the more real when I hear him saying them to someone else. To the person who meant so much to him, she turned his life upside down when they couldn't be together.

Does he look at her and see Willow? Does he see a chance? An opportunity to right the mistakes he feels he made in the past?

Does he see something in her that I can't give him?

I don't have it in me to keep listening. The fear of hearing him say another word chokes me. Flicking the switch on the monitor silence envelopes the room once again. Yet, I still can't move away from the window.

Transfixed, I watch the man I've fallen in love with reach out to hold the hand of another woman. One he's told me he thought he was in love with.

I need to get the hell out of here.

Twenty-seven

TJ

"Do you ever think about us?"

Shit.

I knew as soon as I saw her walking toward me that there was something wrong with Lucy. When she sat in the chair that Bree had just vacated, I had the urge to get up and make an excuse to leave. After a few minutes of uncomfortable small talk, she lapsed into an uncomfortable silence. Until she asked that question.

Do I ever think about it? Yes, but not in the way she's asking.

"Yeah. Luce. I do." I wait a second before I continue, searching for the right words. Whatever it is she's got going on, I don't want to make it worse by saying the wrong thing.

"You fucked me up, Luce." I sigh. "I never really felt much about anyone until you." This conversation has been a long time coming. We've skirted around it in the past, but we've never put it to rest. Is this the right time and place to do it? Probably not, but I want this done so I can move on. I don't want Breeze to feel any insecurities. I don't want her wondering where my head is at.

"Where's this coming from?" I ask, curious about why she's doing this now. She doesn't answer right away, just keeps watching the kids laughing at something the clown is doing.

"I don't know," she finally says, dropping her gaze to her hands as she picks at the label on the beer bottle she's holding. "

guess somewhere in the back of my mind, I always thought it would be me." She shrugs without looking at me. "I thought that when you pulled your head out of your ass, we'd find a way to make it work."

"Luce—" I try to speak, but she cuts me off.

"I know. I moved on first, I met Scott, and I told you I was done, but there was always that tiny little seed in my mind. I thought that it would be us in the end." She sounds so fucking lost, confused by her thoughts. I hate seeing her like this.

"I thought I loved you, and I thought that I lost it all when I lost you." She flinches at my words.

"You *thought* you loved me?" she asks quietly.

"It wasn't until I met Breeze that I realized how wrong I was." I can't help but let my lips tip up in a smile when I think about her, about how she's shown me what love actually is.

"I thought I loved you. But I know now that it was just infatuation. I stood by and watched you live your life from the sideline, Luce. That's not love, and that's not an option with Bree. I want to be part of it; no, I *need* to be part of it. I thought getting over you would be easy with plenty of drink and other women. The thought of touching anyone but Breeze leaves me cold. Damn, I stood here in this very backyard and shook Scott's hand for fuck sake. If Bree ever tried that shit, I'd be locked up for murder," I tell her, laying my feeling out. As I say the words, I realize just how true they are.

"I'm sorry, I shouldn't have dragged all this crap up," she says, her voice thick with emotion. "Scott and I, we're going through some stuff. It'll be fine; I'll be fine. I guess seeing you settled down, happy, it threw me for a minute." She swipes at a tear as it escapes. "I'm so freaking stupid." She huffs out a humorless laugh.

"I don't know what's happening with you guys, but if you need anything at all, even just someone to listen, I'm here," I tell her honestly.

Watching her fall apart is hard, but I know she needs to work through it. When she hits rock bottom, she'll come out the other side. Better and stronger than she was before. Just like I did when I lost her.

Lucy spends a minute or two sitting quietly, composing herself before standing to leave.

"I should go before Breeze comes back," she sniffs. "I don't think she'd appreciate finding me crying over her boyfriend like this."

"You going to be okay?" I ask her.

"I'll be fine." She nods "Thanks." Giving my hand a squeeze, she walks away. She doesn't get very far before she turns back toward me. "I'm happy for you. She's perfect for you and Abel. You have a beautiful family." Her words stun me into silence.

She's right. My family is fucking beautiful.

It isn't until Lucy has gone that I notice Bree hasn't come back yet. Checking my watch, I see she's been gone nearly thirty minutes now. Picking up my empty beer bottle and the baby monitor from the floor, I realize that I didn't hear anything while she was putting Abel down. Usually I get to hear their chattering back and forth as she gets him ready for bed. Unease sits heavy in my gut. Something feels off.

Slowly pushing open the door to the room where Abel is supposed to be sleeping, I half expect to find it empty. Instead, I find my son tucked in tight and fast asleep. His diaper bag is on the floor at the end of the crib. Breeze must have gotten distracted on her way back to me. Heading toward the voices I hear coming from the kitchen, I see Poppy and Elliott lifting a huge cake from its box.

"Hey," Poppy says when she sees me, "how's Breeze feeling?"

"Where is she?" I ask.

"She didn't tell you?" Poppy says, continuing to fuss over the cake. Frustration bites at me. I knew something was wrong.

"Pop," I snap, "tell me where the fuck she went." I know it isn't Poppy's fault, but I can't help it. She wouldn't have left without telling me why, unless there was something very wrong.

"She came out from putting Abel down, and she looked really pale. She said she didn't feel good and that her brother was going to come pick her up."

"And you didn't think to fucking tell me?" I shout.

"I thought you knew!" she shouts back.

"How long?"

"What—"

"How long ago did she leave?" I grit through clenched teeth.

"Not long, maybe twenty minutes ago?" she says, concern tinging her words.

"Can you watch Abel?" I ask, but I'm already moving toward the door.

"Of course. I hope she's okay," she calls out, but I don't wait around to answer. I'm out the door and in my truck within minutes.

I've called her over and over as I drive toward her apartment, but each time it rings out. I can't shake the fear that's taken a grip on me. My mind is working overtime trying to work out why the fuck she'd leave like that.

Pulling my truck into a space in front of the apartment, I see a car parked in front of her garage. I assume it's her brother's. Taking the steps two at a time, I'm about to knock on her door when I hear voices, specifically Breeze. I freeze in place when I hear her say my name. There's a small window next to the door, and it's open a few inches, allowing me to hear what's being said.

"Just calm down and tell me what happened." Her brother's deep voice carries over the sound of her crying.

"What happened was I almost gave up my dream for a guy who was just using me as filler." She cries, and my heart drops. Why the fuck would she think that? "I planned to tell him that I was falling for him, all the while he's telling his ex ... whatever she is, that he still thinks about her. I watched them sitting there, looking like they were made for each other. You should have seen the way she looked at him." She whispers the last part. "I felt like an outsider, again."

I restrain myself from kicking the fucking door open and telling her how wrong she is. I know this is my fault. I should have told her how I felt. I should have made it so there was no room for doubt.

"What did he say when you confronted him?" Her brother sounds like he wants to rip my balls off.

"I didn't. I called you instead." She sniffs.

"Sis, we don't run away from shit. It's not the Lucas way."

"I know, but I just couldn't take it." Her voice sounds muffled, and I assume she's letting her brother hold her. It should be me.

"You were going to stay? For him?"

"For them," she says.

"You'd give up your dreams?" He sounds shocked, but not as shocked as I am right now.

She was going to stay? I've known about her plans to travel from the beginning. I know her dreams, her desire to follow her mom's wish for her. Hearing her say she was going to give all that up for me fills me with a warmth like I've never known. She'd put her life on hold for me and my son.

"No, Asa. My dreams just changed."

Fuck me.

Done with listening to her, I twist the doorknob and step inside. Breeze turns to look at me, shock clear on her face.

"Fucker," Asa mutters as he takes a step toward me. He's a big guy, but I'm bigger. Stopping just inside the doorway, I cross my arms over my chest.

"You were going to stay for me?"

Twenty-eight

BREEZE

I'm struggling to not break down as my brother holds me, but I can feel my emotions getting the best of me. I'm sad, but I'm also disappointed.

The front door opens, and TJ strides into my tiny apartment. Asa's arms tense around me before he pushes me behind him. He takes a step toward TJ, fists clenched. Of all the people that I could have called to collect me from that party, I had to choose my hot-headed older brother. Before Asa can take another step, TJ speaks.

"You were going to stay? For me?"

Of course, he heard me say that. Anger blossoms inside me.

"I don't think that matters anymore, does it?" I can't help but spit the words at him. Our eyes lock, anger blazing in his dark ones. How dare he be angry at me.

"I think it's best if you just leave," Asa says, interrupting our stare off.

"I'm not leaving," TJ states darkly.

"You will if tell you to," Asa says, matching TJ's deadly tone.

"We'll see," TJ retorts.

"Enough!" I shout, causing both heads to swing in my direction. "You'll both leave whenever I tell you to leave." Turning to face TJ, I don't try to hide my feelings anymore; why should I?

"TJ, I have no idea why you're even here," I say, throwing my hands up in frustration.

"Are you kidding me? You fucking left!" he shouts, his face turning a shade of red I've never seen before. "You went to put Abel down for a nap, then you disappeared!"

Something in me snaps, and I can't hold back anymore.

"Because I heard you!" Tears fill my eyes, and there's no point trying to fight them as they fall. It hurts too damn much.

"Baby, let me—" TJ steps toward me again, but Asa cuts him off.

"Back off!"

"I don't want to fight you, but I will if you don't get out of my way," TJ growls at my brother, and his voice is sharp, the sound cutting into me.

"TJ, please. I can't do this," I whisper.

"Tell me what you heard," he demands, but I can't answer. The thought of saying it out loud kills me.

"It doesn't matter—" I try to speak, but it's his turn to cut me off.

"You heard me speaking to Lucy, tell me what I said," he demands, voice raising.

"I heard you tell her you still think about her." I draw in a breath, trying to get the courage to continue. "I heard you tell her how she messed you up. I saw you hold her hand." The last comes out as a whisper.

"That's it?" he demands.

"That's not enough?" I shriek.

"So you missed the rest?" His whole body seems to deflate, the fight draining out of him. "You missed me telling her that I never loved her. That I didn't know what love was until I met you." He says the words so softly that I'm almost sure I've misheard him.

"What?" I breathe.

"It's you, Breeze," he answers. "I told you before, all I see is you."

This time when he moves toward me, Asa doesn't get in his way. Before I realize what's happening, TJ has me swept up in his arms. I bury my face in his neck as tears of relief course down my face. Wrapping my arms around his neck, I hold him as tight as I possibly can.

"I'm an idiot." I cry.

"You are," he agrees, murmuring against the top of my head, "but you're my idiot, okay?"

"Okay." I sniff, unable to control my crying.

A little while later, we're laying on my bed. TJ is on his back, propped up against the pillows, and I'm tucked into his side tightly, my head resting over his heart.

Once TJ managed to calm down my crying, I introduced him to Asa properly. They shook hands and didn't seem to hold any grudges against one another. I promised to call him if I needed anything, then Asa left.

"Is Abel okay?" I ask, breaking the silence of the last few minutes.

"He's fine, baby."

Another few minutes of silence pass, and I'm not sure I can take much more.

"Are we okay?" I ask, bracing for his reply. "I'm sorry for overreacting—"

I don't get the words out before I'm pushed onto my back, and TJ's large frame is hovering over me.

"It's me who should be apologizing. If you had more faith in me, in us, you wouldn't have run."

"No," I interrupt him, "I should have trusted you. You've never given me a reason not to. I think I was just waiting for the other shoe to drop." I hold his beautiful face in both hands and pull him closer for a kiss. I can't believe I tried to walk away from this man. Looking in his eyes, I can see how he feels about me. How was I so blind before? He's shown me every day how he feels. He's let me in to his life, his son's life, and until now, I didn't appreciate how telling of his feelings that is. "You're an amazing man with an amazing child, part of me couldn't understand why you'd want me. It was easier to believe that you just wanted me for now than it was to believe you might want more with me."

"I should have told you, made sure you understood," he murmurs between pecks to my lips.

"You did. I just wasn't listening." I try to concentrate on getting the words out, but it's an impossible task with the weight of him pressing me into my bed. Shifting so he can look into my eyes, TJ rests his head against mine before he speaks again. I don't just hear what he says this time, I feel it.

"I don't just want more with you, sweetheart. I want it all."

The world stops. Time stops. It's just us here in this moment.

"Made a lot of mistakes in my life, baby. I'd make them all again. Every single one if it brought me to you again."

When his lips touch mine, I can taste the urgency. The deep need for me to believe his words. And I do. I don't doubt his feelings, not anymore. Right there, in my bed, I finally open my eyes and my heart and let this man all the way in.

Twenty-nine

TJ

"Fuck, yes," I hiss through gritted teeth. Unable to rip my eyes off the sight in front of me. Breeze's face down in the bed, ass up in the air, and my dick sliding in and out of her pretty pink pussy. "Love how you take me, baby."

Breeze loves it when I talk dirty to her. I can't say it's something I've ever consciously done, but if doing it gets her pussy to convulse like it just did, I'll make sure to do it more often.

My fingers trace down the silky-smooth skin of her back, all the way down to her peachy ass, and I grab a handful of flesh and pump harder. I'm not going to last long like this, she feels too fucking perfect. Sliding out of her wet heat, I get a hint of satisfaction at the disgruntled moan she lets out.

"Don't stop," she begs.

"Patience, baby," I tell her as I flip her over on to her back. She doesn't have time to reply before I'm sliding back inside her. Pure fucking perfection.

My blood is buzzing in my veins. I'm high on her. High on our connection.

Her thighs tighten around me, and I can feel she's right there on the edge. It won't take much to push her over, but I'm in the mood to savor her. Shifting on to my knees, I pull her legs from around my waist and put pressure on the inside of her thighs so she'll spread them wider for me.

Slowing down my thrusts, I drag my cock almost all the way out, before slowly pushing all the way back in.

"Baby ... please..." Breeze groans, her eyes locked on where we're connected.

"What do you need?" I pant, the thin grip I have on my desire about to snap.

"You. Just you." Her eyes flick up to meet mine, and that's all it takes. Leaning over her, I hook one of her legs over the crook of my elbow so I can slide in even deeper.

"Love your pussy, baby," I growl against her lips.

"Harder. TJ ... please," she begs again, and this time I give her what she wants. My hips snap against hers, harder, faster. Driving us toward an ending I know will be explosive for both of us.

Her breath catches, her body going taut for a few seconds before she starts to fall. I feel her, each wave of pleasure that washes over her, rippling through her, and along my cock. Reaching down between us, I run my thumb over her clit, prolonging her pleasure as much as I can.

"TJ!" she gasps "I can't ... It's too much." Her eyes slam shut, but I don't stop; I keep up the punishing rhythm even when her head digs into the pillows. The feel of her nails digging into my biceps only fuels me to push harder into her.

Pounding harder still, I revel in the feel of her. Her warm, wet heat is unreal. The way she squeezes me so fucking tight steals my breath.

I feel the tell-take tingle start at the base of my spine, and I know I'm done. She feels too fucking perfect for me to hold out any longer. I see stars as I finally let go and plant myself as deep inside her as I possibly can, not moving as my orgasm barrels through me.

"I'm pretty sure that's the hardest I've ever come." I breath into Bree's neck a few minutes later. She giggles, causing my semi-hard cock that's still buried deep inside her to stir to life at the feeling. Lifting my head out of her neck, I kiss her softly.

"Let's go get Abel and go home."

Smiling softly, she just nods.

***

"I feel a little silly, going back into your brother's house."

We're in my truck, driving to pick Abel up.

"They won't care. As long as you're okay, they won't give a shit about anything else. Trust me, they've had enough drama of their own over the years." I try to reassure her.

"I know." She's quiet for another minute before asking, "Will Lucy still be there?"

We've only managed a brief conversation, but I've told Bree that whatever is going on with Lucy has nothing to do with me. She's the only one I want, and I'll keep telling her that until I'm blue in the face if that's what it takes for her to believe me.

"I don't know. Please try to forget that shit. Lucy will work her shit out and probably be mortified about how she was today."

"I'll try," she says, squeezing my hand.

Luckily the party is over, and everyone is gone by the time we get to my brother's.

After coming home and getting Abel ready for bed, I watch as Breeze does her usual yoga routine with him. It's crazy how quickly we've settled into a routine. I can't imagine her not being here with us, a part of everything we are.

Asa's words from earlier rattle around in my head.

"You'd give up your dream for him?"

The thought of my Breeze sacrificing her wants for me sits sour in my gut. Can I ask her to do that?

As much as it pains me, I realize that no. I can't.

BREEZE

"You said he was hot, but you didn't say he could be on the cover of Men's Health."

Ava whisper shouts as she passes me in the kitchen. After weeks of her pestering me, I finally caved and brought TJ and Abel to family dinner.

Ava and I are inside clearing away the dishes, while TJ is on the back deck talking sports with Asa, my other brother Beau, and our brother-in-law, Carl. Ava's daughter is sitting on the floor in front of Abel's carrier, pulling faces and making him giggle his infectious laugh.

We've both been incredibly busy with work, and TJ has been with Jonah more and more as the weeks have gone on, so it's taken longer than I'd have liked to arrange tonight.

"I told you he was gorgeous," I laugh. "Wait till you see him holding his son. Your ovaries might not be able to handle it."

"Things are good with you two? He couldn't keep his eyes off you over dinner," she says, handing me a dish to load into the washer.

"Things are very good. It's crazy, but it feels like we've been doing this for years, not just a few months."

"It's not a little weird? You didn't just get a boyfriend; you got a baby at the same time," she asks, but there's no judgement, just curiosity.

"They're a package deal, and I wouldn't have them any other way."

Ava watches me closely, and a slow smile creeps onto her face.

"You love them." It's a quiet statement, not a question.

"I do," I tell her, my voice firm. I know my family had their reservations about my relationship, and I understood why. Not only is TJ a new father, he's also at least ten years older than me. It's never been an issue for us, but my family are natural born worriers, and I knew they would need to see for themselves before they would understand.

"Happy for you, sis. Mom would love him for you."

"You think?" I ask, not realizing until now how much it means to me that she thinks Mom would have liked him. Putting an arm around my shoulder, Ava pulls me in for a quick squeeze.

"Trust me, she would think he's perfect."

I can't help the grin that lights my face. "Good."

The rare, tender moment between us is broken when the back door opens, and the guys all pour into the room. TJ walks straight to me and hooks an arm around my neck and kisses my temple.

"Everything okay?" he asks, and I melt into him. He's the one under the spotlight tonight, but he's asking me if I'm okay.

When he hears his father's voice, Abel lets out a loud shout, letting us know he's ready to be picked up.

"Alright, bud. No need to shout." He squats to unbuckle and lift him up. Once he has him settled on his hip, I turn to look at Ava. She turns to me at the same time, and we both burst out laughing.

"Alright. You can say, "I told you so" now." She giggles.

"What did I miss?" TJ asks, looking between my sister and I as we carry on like a pair of school girls.

"Learn early on that it's better not to ask most of the time," Carl says, making everyone chuckle. He claps TJ on his shoulder and walks over to Ava, kissing her. I love that they're still so affectionate after so many years together. Turning to say something to TJ, I catch him and Asa having a whispered conversation behind my back. They both jump when they realize I've caught them.

"What's going on?" I ask. "Why are you two whispering?" Neither of them answers right away. Asa steps closer to us and surprises me by taking Abel out of TJ's arms.

"I'll let you take over from here," he says to TJ cryptically.

"What's going on?" I demand once more, but I still don't get an answer. Instead, he walks over to the diaper bag that he set in the corner earlier. Rifling through it for a minute, he comes back with a manila envelope in his hands. Looking around the room, I notice that nobody seems in the least surprised by what's going on. In fact, they're all wearing similar goofy smiles.

"I got you something," he says, reaching up to run a hand through his hair. It's his nervous tick. "Well, I got it, but everyone kinda helped out."

My pulse rockets. What the hell has he done that my whole family could have been involved in? Looking at TJ, I can't get a hint of what this could be. His expression is carefully blank.

Reaching for the envelope when he holds it out, I quickly tear it open. My heart hits the floor at what I find inside.

"Flight tickets?" I croak, tears clogging my throat. Why would he do this to me?

"Baby." TJ is in my face immediately, his hands sliding into my hair, and he uses his thumbs to swipe at the tears that are falling. I look up and find concerned eyes looking down at me.

"Why would you do this?" I ask. "Don't you want me here?" His gaze turns pained, and he drops his head down to meet mine.

"We'll give you guys a minute," my sister says as they all leave the room. TJ doesn't drop his eyes from mine, not until the door closes and we're alone. I want to ask questions. I want to know what the hell is going on, but part of me doesn't want to hear his reasons for doing this.

"Breeze, baby ... I stood outside your apartment a few weeks ago and listened to you tell your brother that you were willing to give up your dreams for me. I can't let you do that." I can feel the pain drip from each of his words.

"If you heard me say that, you also heard me say that dreams change. I don't need anything else; I have you. You and Abel are all I need. Why would I need to see Europe when I have you two, right here?" I cry, fisting the sides of his t-shirt, desperate to feel him closer to me.

"But your dreams don't have to change. Don't you see? You can have both. What kind of man would I be if I kept you from doing the one thing you've always wanted to do?"

"I thought you'd be happy I changed my mind."

"You don't get it. I'm fucking thrilled that you'd even consider staying, but I can't let you." Putting a tiny amount of pressure under my chin, TJ tips my head back so he can look at me. "I love you," he says with such a firm clarity. I suck in a shocked breath.

"You love me?"

"I do. More than I ever realized was possible"—he pulls in a big breath— "and that's why I have to let you do this."

Still holding my face in his hands, he drops his mouth to mine. It's not just a kiss, it's a plea for me to understand.

"I need you to do this. For me. So when you come back, I'll know you're coming back having done the one thing you've always wanted. If you don't go, I'll always be waiting for the resentment to grow between us."

I feel like I'm being ripped in two. I want to stay, but I can't deny that the only reason I'd be staying is him.

"I don't want to be without you," I whisper against his lips. His hand slides down my chest, letting it rest over where my heartbeat is going crazy.

"Am I in here?" he asks, and all I can do is nod; I'm scared I'll break down if I try to speak. "Then you're not ever going to be without me."

"It's a few months, baby. We'll speak every day and when you're ready, we'll be here waiting for you." This means something to him, I can feel the desperation in his words.

Sucking in a deep breath, I feel like I'm breaking my own heart when I nod.

"Okay. I'll go"

Thirty-one

TJ

I'm a fucking idiot.

Watching Breeze as she throws her head back and belt out a loud laugh at something one of the kids gathered around her says, I'm once again wondering what the fuck I was thinking encouraging her to leave me. She sits in my backyard, my son on her lap and our families surrounding her, and she looks so fucking perfect it hurts. I watch as Bree and Abel both laugh when Frank, my brother's giant ass dog comes bounding up to them and drops a ball. Picking it up, Bree throws it as far as she can, but Frank is happy to drop down onto the ground next to their picnic blanket. Fuck sake. Even the dog loves her.

She's leaving in less than a week, so she insisted we have everyone over so she can say goodbye to them all at once. There are people everywhere, and I haven't been able to get near her for the last few hours. It's my idea of hell.

But she's had a smile on her face all day, something that's been rare since I surprised her with the plane tickets. Sure, she's gone through the motions and has finally planned where she wants to go and what she wants to see, but her heart hasn't been in it.

Part of me hopes she just refuses to go, but I know deep down that this the best thing for her to do.

"How you holding up?" Hayden says, passing me a beer and dropping into the seat next to me.

"This fucking sucks," I tell him, tipping the beer back and downing half the bottle in a few gulps.

The fucker has the cheek to chuckle at me.

"One day, it will be you getting fucked up over a woman, so laugh it up while you can, dickhead," I tell him, but it just causes him to laugh louder.

"No thanks. I'm happy as I am."

"We'll see," I mutter.

I'm about to go inside for another beer when I hear my name being called. Turning around, I see Breeze is up on her knees on the blanket, Abel on her hip, and she's waving me over.

"You have to see this! Quickly!"

I make my way to the edge of the blanket and just before I get there, she tells me to stop.

"Stay there. You're going to love this." She grins at me, happiness bubbling out of her.

"Let me see then," I say, and my mock impatience causes her to roll her eyes at me.

Shifting Abel so he's on the blanket on all fours, she holds onto his little waist to keep him steady.

"Okay now, gorgeous, let's show daddy what you've learned," she says before kissing my son on his head.

She lets go of him, and he wobbles for a second. Once he's righted himself, he throws himself forward and does an awkward stumble crawl thing toward the dog.

"Holy shit! He's doing it!" I drop to my knees, and Abel changes course and heads toward me instead. It takes everything in me not to scoop him up before he gets to me. When he finally makes it, I throw him up into the air.

"When did you get so grown up?" I ask him as he giggles in my face.

Breeze moves to sit next to us, and I wrap an arm around her, closing the last few inches between us.

"He's been so close to doing it for the last few days, guess all he needed was the right encouragement." She laughs softly. "Today he's crawling, next thing you know he'll be walking, talking, and a whole bunch of other things."

When silence hangs over us, I guess we're both thinking the same thing.

How many of those will she miss while she's away?

"Can I put him down tonight?" Breeze asks when Abel is bathed and ready for bed. "I only have a couple more days and..." She trails off, and I know she's getting emotional. She formed this amazing bond with my boy, and although it started out with me paying her to watch him, I know she loves him.

Just like I know she loves me. It's there, in every look she gives me, it's on the tip of her tongue every day, but she's holding back. I don't blame her. I know I threw her for a loop when I told her to go, but she'll see. She'll see it's for the best. She'll see that a few months out of the lifetime we're going to have together is nothing. At least that's what I keep trying to convince myself.

"You take him, I'll get cleaned up downstairs." I transfer the baby into her arms, kiss his head, then move to kiss her lips.

"Love you," I tell her, like I've told her every day since that first time. I love the flare of her eyes when she hears it, the tiny flush that steals over her cheeks. The infinitesimal draw of breath. It's addictive. She smiles her shy smile, pushes up on her toes and kisses me back. Just like she always does. Yeah, I don't need to hear the words, she shows me every damn day how she feels.

"What's all this?"

Thirty minutes later and I've just finished getting everything ready.

I've recreated our first date. The coffee table is once again pushed to the side, the pillows and snacks on the floor. The only difference is the movie that's playing. Grabbing ahold of her hand, I pull Breeze down onto the makeshift bed.

"I thought we could have a date night," I say, settling her into my side. "But I already picked a movie this time." Lifting the remote, I hit play and the screen comes to life. When she sees the movie I picked, she burst into sweet giggles.

"Dirty Dancing? Really?"

"Well, someone once told me it's one of the best love stories ever told."

"Ahhh. Must have been a very wise person."

"Wiseass more like," I mutter, earning myself a dig in the side. Pulling her close to me, I kiss the top of her head.

"Wanna know a secret?"

"Of course I do." She tilts her head back to see me better.

"I've watched it once before, but I didn't get to see much of it because I had the most beautiful woman I've ever seen sitting next to me, distracting me."

TJ—" she breathes, but I kiss her before she can say anymore. I need to feel her. By the time I drag my lips off hers, her hands are under my shirt, clinging to my back, and she's down to her bra and sleep shorts.

Her kiss-drunk expression, swollen lips, and heaving chest make her the sexiest thing I've ever seen. I need her naked and under me right now. Without wasting another second, I do exactly that.

Thirty-Two

BREEZE

"I better hear from you every single day, or I swear I will fly over to whatever country you're in and kick your ass." Fleur cries as she hugs me tightly.

"Calls, texts, emails, you'll get them all," I promise.

"And you have to promise that you'll at least try to enjoy it, as much as you can, Bree."

I don't want to lie to her, so I just nod.

"Sweetheart, we need to get on the road," TJ says from behind us. Fleur takes a step back and opens her car door.

"Call me when you land. Stay safe!" And then she's gone. I watch her car back out of the driveway and I realize this is it. She's the last of our friends and family to leave. I decided that I only wanted TJ and Abel at the airport with me. Saying goodbye to those two is going to hurt, and the last thing I need is an audience.

"You ready?"

Painting on the fake smile that's become the norm for me, I nod. "Yep, let's do this."

He studies my face for a few seconds, and I know he sees it. As much as I try to hide it, he knows me too well.

All too quickly, we're exiting the freeway and parking at the airport. TJ's had his hand on me in some way all morning. I know this was his idea, and I understand his reasoning, but there's still part of me that's hurting over this whole thing. I can't let myself dwell on it, though. I've said I'll go, so there's no point. Instead, I lift Abel out of his stroller so I can give him one last hug. Kissing his cheeks, I feel the tears start to fall.

"You remember how he likes to be tucked in, right? And which of his bears he likes best? And you'll tell your mom when she watches him?" I start to fret. I've been the one looking after Abel for the last four months. It's been me who's fed and cared for him. It's me who knows what he needs.

"He's crawling now, will she be able to chase him?" Panic hits me. I can't do this. I can't leave my boy.

"Baby,"—TJ grabs my face—"we've got this. I promise, we'll be fine."

Of course they will. TJ is his dad. I know this, but the panic is taking over.

"I'm sorry. I'm being stupid." I face plant into his chest, reveling in the feel of him, the smell of him.

"It's not stupid, baby."

"I'm going to miss you both."

"We'll miss you too," he whispers against my lips before he kisses me deeply. Abel, never one to like being left out, is soon slapping a wet fist against our faces.

"I'm sorry, gorgeous boy," I croon, hugging him as tightly as he'll allow.

"Promise me you'll look after Daddy while I'm gone? Be a good boy, and eat all your dinners, okay?" He looks at me as if he understands every word I've just said. I've no idea how I'm going to get through the days without seeing him.

Reaching into his jacket pocket, TJ pulls out a small white envelope. "Here, Abel wants you to take this," he says, passing it to me as he lifts the baby out of my arms.

"Abel does, huh?"

"Yeah. He didn't want you to miss him too much," he says, and I smile genuinely for the first time in what feels like forever.

Ripping open the envelope, I pull out a small photograph. My heart squeezes in my chest, and tears fill my eyes yet again when I see my two favorite people staring back at me. I remember taking this picture. Just last week we'd packed a picnic and taken Abel for a day at the zoo. TJ strapped him into a carrier on his chest, and I'm pretty sure it's the hottest he's ever looked. I snapped the picture when they were looking at something in the distance. They're standing in profile, and Abel looks so much like TJ it's crazy.

"I know you have it on your phone, but I thought you'd like a real copy too."

"I love it," I tell him, throwing my arms around him and Abel.

We stand there for as long as we can, until I'm at risk of missing my flight. Putting Abel back into his stroller, TJ pulls me in for one last kiss.

"I'm going to miss you so fucking much," he rasps.

Emotion clogs my throat and again, all I can do is nod.

"I'll be here. When you come home, I'll be here waiting." He drags me closer, pressing me against his body tightly.

This time the kiss is desperate. He breathes me in. And I let him.

When he drags his mouth away, he drops his forehead to meet mine.

"I need you to know, this is for you. For us. I'm breaking my own heart here, baby."

"I get it," I tell him, lifting my hands to run through his hair. "I really do."

"Have fun and stay safe. For us," he rasps, his eyes searching mine.

"I'll try."

And then I'm walking away. With each step I take, I wait for him to call for me. I wait for him to stop me, for him to say it.

If he says it, I'll stay. All I need to hear is those three little words.

"Baby, please stay."

But he doesn't say a single word.

I can't look back, I can't stop. Not when I feel his eyes burning into my back as I walk through security. Not when I hear Abel yelling for me.

I don't stop until I'm at the departure gate. Once I know he can't see me, I let the tears flow once again.

TJ

I should be celebrating.

Tonight, Jonah won his first big fight. Everything we worked for, every sacrifice made just paid off. But I just can't bring myself to be happy. There's a party happening around me, but instead I'm sitting alone in my office nursing a bottle of bourbon. All I can do is stare at my phone, willing it to ring.

It's been two weeks since she left. Two weeks of hell.

Watching her walk away from me in the airport took every ounce of strength not to run after her. To tell her that I'm an idiot. That I wanted her to stay.

Instead, I made her go.

Two weeks of phone calls, Skype chats, and FaceTime just isn't enough. Not when I see the sadness etched in her face still. Sure, there's been moments when she's looked happy, but seeing her forcing a smile for me whenever we speak is killing me.

I didn't realize the small things I'd miss until I didn't have them anymore. Being able to lean over and kiss her good morning. I want to hold her hand in front of our friends. I want to laugh with her, make fun of her when she messes up.

I want to love on her in front of the whole world, but instead we're thousands of miles apart, and it's all my fault.

"What are you doing hiding in here?" The door to my office opens, and my dad walks in, taking a seat in front of my desk. "You should be celebrating. You did a hell of a job with Jonah."

"Just trying to get ahold of Bree." I wave the phone at him.

"Where is she now? How's she liking it so far?"

"She's in Rome for the next few days, then she's heading to Greece." I sigh "She says she's enjoying it, but she's a shit liar," I tell him. "I see it when she FaceTimes; she's trying, but she's just ... off." He remains quiet, knowing I'm not done speaking. He waits patiently for me to get my thoughts in order.

"Did I do the right thing?" I ask the question that's kept me awake for weeks now.

"You did what you thought was best."

"For her? Or for me?" I scoff.

"Stop beating yourself up; you did what you thought was best for both of you," he says sharply.

"Dad—"

"What are you doing, son?" softening his tone.

"What kind of question is that? I'm here! I'm working every damn day!" I slam my glass down on the desk, ignoring the liquid that splashes over the side. "I'm trying to be the best I can fucking be for my son."

"You remember when I was sick?" His question silences me.

It was over ten years ago, but it isn't something I'm ever likely to forget. Keir and I were just finishing college, he was going to the NFL, I was working my way up to fighting professionally. Then Dad got sick. Cancer. We'd rallied, got him through appointments and did what had to be done. But I'd never, not as long as I lived forget how he looked when he was fighting to beat that disease. How my giant of a father looked broken and frail.

"You think I was lying in that bed, sure as heck I was going to die, regretting the weekends I spent at home with you boys? Do you think I was laid up thinking I wish I'd worked more? Missed date nights with your mother?"

"I get what you're saying bu—"

"No buts about it, son. Nothing in this life is promised." He stands, ready to leave as if he didn't just knock me on my ass.

"He's right," my brother interrupts from where he's leaning against the door. I didn't even notice him coming in.

"What is this? Some kind of intervention?" I ask, knowing if they're both cornering me in here, there's something they want to say, something they want me to hear.

"Hell yes, it is," Keir says, standing next to our dad, arms crossed over his chest and his face determined.

"It's too late," I mutter, tipping what's left of the glass of bourbon back and relishing the burn it leaves behind.

"Is it?" my dad asks quietly.

"Brother, if you only ever take one thing I say seriously, let it be this," Keir says, leveling me with the serious expression on his face, "Don't waste time like I did. It's never too late."

It's never too late.

Thirty-four

BREEZE

"Pick up, pick up, pick up," I mutter impatiently at my phone. I've been trying to get through to TJ since last night, and for some reason none of my FaceTime calls are working. The internet connection is so shitty here. Luckily, I've managed to speak to him through text messages and an all too brief phone call, but it's been three days since I last saw him and Abel. Seeing them on a tiny screen doesn't compare to the real thing, but it's better than nothing.

I give up after trying to get through to him one last time. Sending him a text asking him to call me, I put the phone into the pocket of my shorts and head down to the beach.

I've been away for three weeks. Twenty-one days.

And I begrudgingly admit that TJ was probably right to force me to do this. I've seen so much, experienced so many things. If I hadn't have come, I'd probably would have always wondered what I might have missed.

When I landed in London, I was desperate to turn around and get the first flight home. My first day there, I walked the streets and hated every step I took. It wasn't until I started doing the things my mom had talked about wanting to do that my attitude adjusted. As I ticked the sights off the list she'd unknowingly made for me, I'd found an appreciation for TJ and his determination to get me here.

With new eyes, and new resolve, I vowed to make the most of my time here.

I've seen Paris and the Eiffel Tower lit up at night.

I've seen the Sagrada Familia in Barcelona.

I've seen the Vatican and the Parthenon.

And I've done it all with part of me missing.

All my life I wanted to leave Savannah, to travel the world, because I wanted more. More than feeling trapped like my mom felt. But I realize now I feel the opposite of that when I'm with him. With them.

I felt like I was where I was meant to be. And I fucking miss them. With everything in me, I miss them.

"Good evening, Miss Breeze," one of the waiters, Spiro, says as I climb on to the stool and drop my purse on the worn wooden bar. I've been at a small beach resort on one of the Greek islands for the last few days, and aside from the shitty internet connection, it's one of my favourite places I've been so far. Accepting a small beer from the bartender, I turn around on my seat so I'm facing the ocean. Closing my eyes, I let the sea breeze wash over me. The sun is close to setting, and the burnt orange sky is turning inky at its edges. The water gently laps at the rocks that line the shore.

"It's a beautiful night, yes?" Spiro asks from behind me.

"It really is." I sigh, not taking my eyes off the view. I watch as the sun sets, kissing the ocean as it goes. As it disappears below the horizon, I'm hit with a fresh wave of loneliness. Another day here, on my own.

Without TJ. Without Abel.

It's taken me leaving them to realize something. I can be anything I want to be, go anywhere in the world I want to go. But the truth is, I only want to be his. To be with them.

I can't help but wonder if this is what my mom would have really wanted for me, for any of her kids.

I realize that what I always thought of as her dreams, were not just hers. She wanted to travel, to see the world, but more than that, she really wanted to do it with my dad at her side.

What's the point of seeing all these amazing things without the one you love by your side? How did I ever think I'd be able to do this while TJ sits at home, his life on pause until I'm done roaming.

What the hell am I doing here?

I need to go home. Now.

Sweeping my purse from the table, I yank out a few euros. Throwing them on the bar to pay for my drink, I shout a goodbye to Spiro before turning to run to my room. I need to find a decent computer because I'm booking a flight home. Right now.

Searching for the room key as I rush up the steps to my room, a loud squeal stops me in my tracks. I drop the purse I was just digging in as my head flies up.

I know that sound.

My eyes land on the most beautiful thing I've ever seen, more beautiful than any of the places I've been or things I've seen over these long few weeks.

My boys. They came for me.

My breath stutters, and my hands fly to my mouth to stop the sob that threatens, but it's pointless.

TJ is here. If I reach out, I can touch him. He's here, and he's holding Abel.

When I don't move, he walks toward me. Abel isn't patient either, and he stretches his chubby arms toward me. He's grown so much. FaceTime calls haven't shown me just how much he's changed.

"Are you really here?" I sob. My emotions bubbling out of me.

"We're really here, baby." TJ chuckles

Lifting Abel into my arms, I pepper his little face with kisses as TJ pulls me into his arms.

I melt into them both.

"What are you doing here?" I finally manage to say around the tears that won't stop.

"I decided it was time to stop being an idiot." He laughs lightly, and the sound fills me up.

"I'm here because I love you, and you love me," he tells me resolutely. "I'm here because I fucking missed you," he says against my lips. "I missed not being able to kiss you anytime I wanted. I missed sleeping next to you. I missed every fucking thing about you, sweetheart." He kisses me before I can say anything in reply. He kisses me so deeply, so urgently.

"I'm here because nothing makes sense without you."

We might be thousands of miles away from Savannah, but I've never felt more at home than I do right now.

Epilogue

TJ
Two years later

"Shhh!" Abel says, slamming a sticky hand over my lips when I open my mouth to speak. "Mama sweeping," he tells me sternly, like I can't see Bree curled up asleep on the bed in front of me.

"I know, bud," I whisper back, pulling his hand away. Closing the bedroom door softly, I drop Abel into a seat.

"See my baby?" he asks, leaning over the crib that's pulled up next to the bed.

"Careful, bud." I stop him from poking the sleeping baby. "Your baby brother is sleepy." But it's too late, wide, gray eyes blink up at me from the crib. Eyes identical to how Abel's were at a few days old.

Lifting our baby out of the crib, I settle into the chair next to Abel.

"Baby!" he says, making grabby hands like he expects me to hand over his new brother.

"When Mama wakes up, you can hold him, okay?"

"Hmmkay," he says, jutting out a little lip in protest. Placing the new baby against my chest, I wrap my arm around Abel and pull him in closer, reveling in the feeling that holding both of my sons close brings.

Who the fuck would have thought that I'd ever be a father to two amazing little boys like this?

The last two years have been a dream come true. A dream I didn't realize I could have until Breeze.

Without a doubt, taking that flight to surprise her was the best decision I ever made in my life.

We'd ended up spending another month finishing the tour of Europe that she'd planned. Doing it with Abel in tow wasn't easy, but it was more than worth it to see Bree lit up with excitement.

It took approximately fifteen minutes after arriving home in the US for me to convince her to move in with us officially.

It was approximately another five minutes after that, that I had my ring on her finger.

She was my wife within a month.

I'll never forget the sight of her walking toward me that day. We were married in our backyard, next to the lake she loves so much. Wearing a long white dress, her hair once again pink, she carried Abel down the aisle with her.

It took much longer to give Abel a sibling than either of us wanted.. Not for lack of trying, it just didn't happen for us right away. Yet another day I'll never forget, the day she stood in our bathroom, little white stick in her hand, and tears running down her face. I didn't think I could love her any more than I already did, but her giving me a chance to be part of all the things I missed with Abel, that was a gift. One I cherish every fucking day.

Somewhere along the way, Abel had grown. What felt like overnight, he suddenly started walking and talking. His first word was dada. I'm man enough to admit that the sound of that almost brought me to my knees.

His second word was mama, and I felt that word too. Abel will grow up knowing all about Willow, I wouldn't have it any other way, but Breeze *is* his mother in every way possible. In every way that matters.

She adopted him when we married, but that piece of paper makes zero difference to how she loves him.

"Look at my three favorite boys." Bree's sleepy voice brings me out of my thoughts. She looks tired but still so fucking beautiful. Looking at her now, you'd never think she gave birth just a few days ago. Fifteen hours of labor, an almost nine-pound baby, and she looks like that? Yeah, I'm a lucky guy.

Leaning over, I slide my hand behind her head, into her hair, and pull her in for a kiss.

"Morning, beautiful," I whisper, not taking my lips off hers.

"Mama!" Abel yells, startling the baby and interrupting the sweet moment.

"Hey, my gorgeous boy." Breeze laughs as he launches himself at the bed.

"My baby," he says once he's settled next to her, making the same grabby hands motion again.

"We need to give him a name. Before Abel convinces him it's just baby," I joke as I put him gently in Abel's waiting arms.

"What about Theodore? Theo for short," my wife says, staring at me with tired, but bright eyes.

My heart squeezes in my chest.

"Baby..." I can't find the words to tell her what it means to me that she would even think of giving him my name.

It's taken a long time, but over the years Bree has shown me it's okay to let go of the guilt I carried over Willow and almost missing out on knowing my son. I can't change my past actions, but I can and have tried my best to be a good husband, brother, and above all, father.

Breeze telling me she wants to name our son after me is the validation I'll probably always be searching for on some level.

BREEZE
Three years later

"Boys!" yelling out the kitchen window, I see three little heads turn my way. "Daddy will be home in ten minutes. Toys away or you're not going on the boat!"

Abel jumps from his seat and immediately starts to pack away the game he was playing. My boy is almost six-years-old, and he is the sweetest soul. I watch a while longer as he moves around the table to help Theo with his mess too. Just like Abel, Theo is the spitting image of his father. From the dark hair, to the even darker eyes, they look exactly like him, all our boys do. Where Abel is the sweet and affectionate one, Theo is a brute. He'd rather wrestle than cuddle, but that's okay. It just makes his rare shows of affection all the sweeter when they happen.

"Mama!" my baby boy shouts at me, a huge grin on his face. Gabe was a surprise baby for us. After a year of trying for a baby before we had Theo and all the heartache that came with it, I was unsure if trying for a third child would ever be something I could do.

Turns out, it didn't matter what I thought because despite being on birth control and breastfeeding Theo, I'd gotten pregnant again within months.

Three boys under six definitely isn't for the faint of heart. They keep me so busy that I hardly have a minute to myself. The only yoga I get to do these days is here at home with my boys.

I wouldn't change a second of my life for anything, though.

Tightening the straps on Abel's life jacket, I'm about to lift him into the boat when he grabs a hold of my arm.

"Love you, Mama," he says before turning and climbing into the boat by himself, completely unaffected, like he didn't just kick my world of its axis.

"Love you, Mama!" the rest of my boys shout as the boat starts to move away.

My heart is fit to burst.

"Love you, babies!" I shout in reply.

"Love you, wife!" TJ cups his hand around his mouth so his voice will carry across the water. The grin on his face is blinding.

I have no idea what I did to deserve this life, but I thank God every single day that I get to live it.

FLAWED LOVE
BOOK ONE

She was my first love.

She was my everything.

We were college sweetheart. The all-American couple.

Until the big time came calling.

Misunderstandings and miscommunications lead to broken hearts and broken trust.

But fate throws me a second chance when our paths cross again.

Now Poppy has to decide if she's ready to take another try at forever with me, or if the past is better left behind us.

I know this is my final down. My last opportunity to make it right, but Poppy's going to need a little more convincing.

Throwing out a Hail Mary, I'll give it all I've got.

With a little luck, this time I may just be able to Score.

FLAWED LOVE
BOOK TWO

He's my best friends' brother.

She's not over her ex.

Elliott.

I should have seen it coming, my world being shattered by the man that was supposed to love me. But I didn't and now I'm trying to find the pieces of me he left behind.

Duke.

I can't fix her, not when I'm just as broken as she is. I should leave her alone, she's too good for me. But, fighting the attraction that pulls us together is getting harder every day.

It doesn't take long until we're a tangle of limbs and pleasures.

No promises are made, no guarantees.

Just a vow to keep our hearts out of the bedroom.

Simple, right?

Except, now we both have to try and avoid getting cut on each other's broken parts.

Available in Kindle Unlimited

Acknowledgments

Brenda - I say it all the time, but I'd be lost without you. Thank you for everything. I'm excited to see what the future holds for us.

My Alpha readers – Nicole and Lily. Thank you for everything you do and for listening to me when I'm whining.

My beta readers – Julia and Leeann. Thank you for taking the time to read this when it was a rough draft. Your feedback is invaluable.

Cornelia – thank you for letting me steal that opening line. It was exactly the line I didn't know I needed.

Silla – thank you for not hating me when I miss my deadline. Thank you for being so patient when even I can't remember what the heck it was I was trying to say.

My cover artist, **Mary Ruth** - I have no idea how you still work me after I changed this cover image approximately six thousand times. Thank you for always making my vision come to life.

My reader group and my review team – LOVE YOU ALL! Thank you for all your support.

Bloggers and Bookstagramers – thank you all for the love and support you've shown me. It blows my mind when I see one of you sign up to review one of my books. I know and appreciate how much hard work you guys put in to blogging and I can't thank you enough.

A NOTE FROM THE Author

Readers, I can't thank you enough for picking up Struck. I hope you enjoyed TJ and Bree's story as much as I enjoyed writing it.

This story is one that had been in my mind long before any of the others in this series and I'm so happy I finally get to share it.

I'm sad to be leaving the Flawed Love series behind, these characters have taken over my life for the last year. I've already asked if there will be more from these characters and I can say that yes, I will definitely be writing more in this world as soon as my schedule allows.

Again, thank you for taking the time to read and I hope you'll consider leaving a review.

ABOUT THE

A long-time lover of all things romance, Emma Louise is a book blogger turned debut writer. She's a die-hard bibliophile, addicted to tea and speaks fluent sarcasm. She lives with her husband, three children and overgrown puppy in South Wales, UK.

Having been an avid reader for as long as she can remember, she's recently decided to try her hand at writing a love story of her own.

Amazon: https://amzn.to/2PSaocd

Bookbub: https://bit.ly/2wu8iaA

FB: https://bit.ly/2wrGYK4

Reader group: https://goo.gl/w6aHvo

IG: https://bit.ly/2wxeMV9

Newsletter: https://bit.ly/2NxOzNI

Printed in Great Britain
by Amazon

39315912R10116